"I'm Twenty-Nine Years Old And I've Never Had A Lover In My Whole Life."

"You mean you're a…you've never…"

"No." Del's voice got softer and the animation drained from her features. "I've never."

"Why?" How on earth could a woman as beautiful as Del still be a virgin? He knew he should respond like a friend, a co-worker, but his body had other ideas. Ruthlessly, he shoved away the surge of desire that rose.

"Well, look at me. I don't exactly dress like a guy's fantasy."

"So? You could have found someone if you'd wanted."

"That's just it. I never wanted. Until now."

"Why now? And if you're interested in a relationship, why not go about it in a more conventional way instead of meeting someone here, in this bar?"

"A relationship? No. I just need to get this over with, see what the fuss is all about."

"Okay. If you're so damn determined to lose your virginity tonight, then it might as well be with me."

Dear Reader,

As expected, Silhouette Desire has loads of passionate, powerful and provocative love stories for you this month. Our DYNASTIES: THE DANFORTHS continuity is winding to a close with the penultimate title, *Terms of Surrender,* by Shirley Rogers. A long-lost Danforth heir may just have been found—and heavens, is this prominent family in for a big surprise! And talk about steamy secrets, Peggy Moreland is back with *Sins of a Tanner,* a stellar finale to her series THE TANNERS OF TEXAS.

If it's scandalous behavior you're looking for, look no farther than *For Services Rendered* by Anne Marie Winston. This MANTALK book—the series that offers stories strictly from the hero's point of view—has a fabulous hero who does the heroine a very special favor. Hmmmm. And Alexandra Sellers is back in Desire with a fresh installment of her SONS OF THE DESERT series. *Sheikh's Castaway* will give you plenty of sweet (and naughty) dreams.

Even more shocking situations pop up in Linda Conrad's sensual *Between Strangers.* Imagine if you were stuck on the side of the road during a blizzard and a sexy cowboy offered *you* shelter from the storm…. (Hello, are you still with me?) Rounding out the month is Margaret Allison's *Principles and Pleasures,* a daring romp between a workaholic heroine and a man she doesn't know is actually her archenemy.

So settle in for some sensual, scandalous love stories…and enjoy every moment!

Melissa Jeglinski

Melissa Jeglinski
Senior Editor, Silhouette Desire

Please address questions and book requests to:
Silhouette Reader Service
U.S.: 3010 Walden Ave., P.O. Box 1325, Buffalo, NY 14269
Canadian: P.O. Box 609, Fort Erie, Ont. L2A 5X3

FOR
SERVICES
RENDERED

ANNE MARIE
WINSTON

Silhouette®
Desire

Published by Silhouette Books
America's Publisher of Contemporary Romance

SILHOUETTE BOOKS

ISBN 0-373-76617-3

FOR SERVICES RENDERED

This edition published by arrangement with Harlequin Books S.A.

® and TM are trademarks of Harlequin Books S.A., used under license. Trademarks indicated with ® are registered in the United States Patent and Trademark Office, the Canadian Trade Marks Office and in other countries.

Visit Silhouette Books at www.eHarlequin.com

Printed in U.S.A.

Books by Anne Marie Winston

Silhouette Desire

Best Kept Secrets #742
Island Baby #770
Chance at a Lifetime #809
Unlikely Eden #827
Carolina on My Mind #845
Substitute Wife #863
Find Her, Keep Her #887
Rancher's Wife #936
Rancher's Baby #1031
Seducing the Proper Miss Miller #1155
*The Baby Consultant #1191
*Dedicated to Deirdre #1197
*The Bride Means Business #1204
Lovers' Reunion #1226
The Pregnant Princess #1268
Seduction, Cowboy Style #1287
Rancher's Proposition #1322
Tall, Dark & Western #1339
A Most Desirable M.D. #1371
Risqué Business #1407
Billionaire Bachelors: Ryan #1413
Billionaire Bachelors: Stone #1423
Billionaire Bachelors: Garrett #1440
Billionaire Bachelors: Gray #1526
Born To Be Wild #1538
The Marriage Ultimatum #1562
The Enemy's Daughter #1603
For Services Rendered #1617

Silhouette Books

Broken Silence
"Inviting Trouble"

Family Secrets
Pyramid of Lies

*Butler County Brides

ANNE MARIE WINSTON

RITA® Award finalist and bestselling author Anne Marie Winston loves babies she can give back when they cry, animals in all shapes and sizes and just about anything that blooms. When she's not writing, she's managing a house full of animals and teenagers, reading anything she can find and trying *not* to eat chocolate. She will dance at the slightest provocation and weeds her gardens when she can't see the sun for the weeds anymore. You can learn more about Anne Marie's novels by visiting her Web site at www.annemariewinston.com.

For the Out-of-Control Croppin' Crew:
Kathy, Connie, Janis, Judi, Vick and Susan
It was a sultry night.

One

"Please tell me this is the last one."

Sam Deering linked both hands above his head and stretched his powerful arms. He had kinks in his back from sitting so long, exactly the kind of thing his physical therapist would give him hell for, but he really needed to get somebody into the new position so he had to finish the interviews today. He dropped his glasses on top of the stack of paper before him and stood, stretching his left leg. It had never been the same since he'd been shot, but it was a lot better than anyone expected, so he supposed he couldn't complain.

"You okay?" Del Smith, the vice president of Protective Services, Incorporated, looked up from the résumé she was reviewing, her heavily lashed brown eyes focusing on him.

"Yeah." He picked up his glasses and resettled them on his nose, then nodded at the door. "Let's get this over with." It had been an exciting ride over the past few years, he thought. PSI might have started out small, but it was making up for it now. About a month ago, he'd realized they needed an assistant for their in-house undercover consultant to handle the amount of work they were getting. He liked the fact that his Virginia-based company could respond to so many different needs in people's lives, from kidnappings to home-security analyses to bodyguard services, but it kept him on his toes.

Del and him, he corrected himself. Without her, he might never have been able to put this all together.

"This is the last one." Del's husky voice sounded as relieved as he was. She laid a neat file before him on his desk, picking up the previous one at the same time. "Here's the next interview."

Sam flipped open the file, casually riffling through it as he watched her from beneath his lashes. "What do you think so far?"

Del shrugged slender shoulders beneath the oversize man's work shirt that was part of her standard code of dress. Beneath the open shirt she wore a PSI T-shirt that probably would fit Sam. He suspected there were some decent breasts under those sloppy casual clothes, but in seven years, he'd never once seen her in anything other than her jeans and shirts or a shapeless black jacket and pants she wore when they entertained clients. It wasn't exactly the kind of thing he could ask about, either. *So, Del, what size jugs you got under that shirt?* No, probably not a good idea.

Unaware of his thoughts, Del shook her head as she arranged papers in front of her own seat. "The Sanders man probably would be competent, but he didn't show me anything special, if you want the truth."

He nodded, forcing himself to focus on the potential employees they'd spent the afternoon interviewing. "I agree. Maybe we'll get lucky on the last one."

Del gave him a small smile as she turned to walk to the doorway. "Maybe."

As she strode across the floor in the no-nonsense style he associated with Del, Sam watched her go. He knew she was slender beneath the baggy jeans and shapeless shirt, but the clothes left him guessing at details. Over the years, he'd become obsessed with trying to catch her in positions that might give him a hint of what lay beneath those layers.

Today, as always, her long, shiny brown hair was braided into a single thick rope that hung from the hole in the back of the baseball cap she always wore and as she walked, it twitched from side to side, brushing across her butt rhythmically, capturing his gaze as surely as if she were stripping in front of him. What would that mane of waist-length hair look like loose and flowing around her shoulders? Hard to believe that in nearly seven years of working in each other's pockets every day, he'd never seen her with it down.

He shifted in his chair, glad he was sitting down. He doubted any of his employees had any idea how his vice president turned him on and he wanted to keep it that way. It wasn't as if he had any intention of acting on it, after all.

No, the last thing he needed was any sort of entanglement with a woman. PSI was the only mistress he had time for. A flesh-and-blood woman would never be content with the long hours he put in, the occasional urgent summons and instant response that certain kinds of cases required.

The door of his office opened again and Del ushered in a tall woman in a severe dark jacket and pants with a white button-down shirt. The jacket was a boxy, unconstructed cut and as he assessed her, he'd bet that it had been made to conceal a sidearm, although she wasn't carrying today.

Del took her seat at Sam's side with a second file. "This is Karen Munson," she said. "Karen, Sam Deering, the president of PSI."

She turned her attention to Sam for a moment. "Ms. Munson has a Criminal Justice degree from Penn State. She started as a beat cop in Miami, worked her way up to Homicide investigations and then applied to the FBI. Her background includes criminal profiling, kidnapping investigations and long-term deep-cover assignments."

"Call me Karen," the woman said, smiling at him. There was no hint of flirtation in the smile, and no hint that she recognized him as anything other than the head of the firm.

Good. The last thing he needed was an employee blabbing his whereabouts to the press. He'd had enough media attention nine years ago to last a lifetime. Even Del didn't know about his past.

He'd considered telling her a time or two, back in the early days when even the easiest of physical tasks had been such an obvious struggle for him. But she'd never asked how he'd been hurt, simply did what she could to lighten his load. And in recent years, he'd improved so much that he sometimes even forgot he'd been shot.

"Why did you get out of undercover work, Ms. Munson?" he asked, glancing at the file.

"I had a child," she said. "I wanted more regular hours."

"You might not always get them here," he warned.

She nodded. "I understand. I've read the information you gave me. But my circumstances have changed now and I have no time constraints anymore."

"None? No child care?"

Karen Munson's mouth compressed into a thin line. She looked away for a moment and he saw her take a deep, fortifying breath. "My son has passed away," she said quietly. "Frankly, Mr. Deering, the busier you can keep me, the happier I'll be." She leaned forward, all business again. "As you can see, I have management experience as well as expertise in a number of the areas you indicate you need."

The interview went on for another thirty minutes, longer than he'd spent with the other three applicants who had cleared the background checks and job-description requirements. When it ended, he'd hired Karen Munson as an assistant to his undercover ops team leader.

She shook his hand, then Del's, and Del led her to her office to give her some paperwork to fill out over the weekend. As she shut the door behind them, his intercom beeped. Punching an open channel, he said, "What's up, Peg?"

Peggy Doonen was Del's assistant and had been manning the front office during the interview.

"It's quittin' time, that's what's up!" Peggy's boisterous good humor boomed around the room. "I thought you said we had a light weekend coming up."

"We do. What's your rush?" Sam didn't generally engage in banter with his employees but Peggy was a force of nature, the office's self-appointed morale officer, class clown and party planner. He'd actually made part of her job description "employee satisfaction" a couple of years ago, and she was worth every penny of the increase. The office was a pleasant, friendly working environment, his employees a close-knit team that generally ran amazingly smoothly despite all the different personalities.

"It's Del's birthday is what's the rush," she informed him. "And we're taking her out to dinner tonight. So unless you've got something important going on in there, set her free. Matter of fact, why don't you relax a little for once and come along with us?"

"No, thanks." The refusal was automatic. "That might inhibit some people."

"That's ridiculous," Peggy opined. "If you change your mind, we'll be at O'Flaherty's Irish Pub. We're meeting at six."

"Have a good time," he said automatically. Del's birthday. For a moment, he felt vaguely guilty. She'd worked for him since he'd opened the firm seven years ago, was his most trusted employee…and he didn't even know it was her birthday. It wasn't as if he didn't have access to the information, either. He'd just never bothered to learn.

Then he shrugged it off. That was part of Peggy's job, making sure employee birthdays were recognized. She sent cards from the firm on which he dutifully scribbled his signature when she thrust them under his nose. She organized lunch or dinner get-togethers to celebrate, although he'd never attended—

His intercom buzzed again. "Yo," he said, punching a button.

"Ms. Munson's gone. She'll be here Monday at nine," Del's voice said. "I'm heading out, too, unless there's anything else you need."

"No. See you Monday."

"Have a good weekend. See you Monday."

"Hey, Del?"

"What?"

"Happy birthday."

"Oh." She sounded surprised and pleased, and he mentally thanked Peggy for clueing him in. "Thank you."

"I would sing, but we'd both be sorry," he told her.

"We'll pretend you already did," she suggested. "Thanks for the lovely serenade." She chuckled, a warm, husky sound that vibrated pleasantly through him. He'd always liked making her laugh, though she did it rarely. Del was one of the most focused people he'd ever known when her mind was engaged on a problem. And in their line of work, problems were commonplace.

"Have a good weekend," he said.

"You, too." Her intercom clicked off.

He stood there for a moment, wishing she didn't have to leave. Then he shook himself. *Don't be ridiculous, Deering. You don't need to get involved with anyone who works for you.*

That was assuming Del would even be interested in him, anyway. As far as he knew, she had never dated anyone from work. Hell, he couldn't remember her ever speaking about her personal life, so he really didn't know whether she dated at all. She'd been single when he hired her and he was pretty sure she still was. No husband would put up with the hours Del spent at work. She was with him way more than half her waking hours in any given week.

He was on his way home when the idea popped into his head and wouldn't go away. *Why not? Peggy invited you,* he reminded himself.

Yeah, but she didn't really mean it.

Sure she did. Peggy doesn't say things she doesn't mean.

The other employees wouldn't like it.

How would you know? You're always invited but you never go.

All right. Fine. So he'd go one time just to see what all the birthday hoopla was about. And because it was Del. After all, she was his second in command, and he really should recognize all the work she did for him. He swung the car off the Capital Beltway toward Fairfax, where he knew O'Flaherty's was located not far from Tyson's Corner Mall.

He glanced at his watch. Seven-fifteen. He'd be late, but that was good, wasn't it? This way, his employees would see that he just stopped to offer his best wishes, not to cramp their party style. And they'd have finished dinner by now.

He parked and walked into the Irish pub. He was barely through the front door before he saw them. There were three round tables crammed full of PSI people.

No, that wasn't right. There was a slender redhead who wasn't one of his employees. She was so unslender in one particular spot that she must have had implants, he decided. She was snuggling against Gerald Walker, a former federal agent who headed up the security-analysis team. Walker had been through a bitter divorce about a decade ago. Sam knew this because one night shortly after PSI had opened he'd called Walker to come in on an after-hours consult and the man staggered in with one of the worst hangovers Sam had ever seen on someone still standing.

"Saw my ex today for the first time in a couple of years," Walker had explained. "It was either drink or put my fist through a wall."

Sam shook his head at the memory as he wove through the crowd. There was one other woman he didn't know with the group, a petite female with a wealth of chestnut hair softly waving around her shoulders and falling down her back. She wore a strappy little black dress that exposed slim, muscled arms and shoulders and a generous amount of cleavage. Wow. None of his employees looked like *that* in a little black dress.

She had her face turned away from him, talking to the firm's accountant with whom she must have come. He couldn't see if the face matched that truly delectable body. Still, he wondered idly what a woman like that was doing with the chubby, bookish accountant.

But…where was Del? His steps slowed as he realized the birthday girl wasn't in the crowd.

"Sam! Hey, Sam, glad you could make it!" Peggy spotted him and stood up, one hand waving madly. "Look, everyone, it's Sam."

He ducked his head and made for the table, miserably aware that half the people in the place had turned to look at him. Damn! What a dumb idea.

Why hadn't he talked himself out of this? It was true he hadn't been recognized in some years now, but this would be the perfect place for it. He came to such restaurants and bars so rarely that he actually couldn't remember the last time he'd been out for a purely social function.

He forged through the room to his group's tables. Peggy already had requisitioned an extra chair and everyone at her table scooched over so he could join them. Peggy had placed the chair beside hers. Directly across the table from him sat Grover and one of the strangers.

Only when she lifted her head and looked across the table at him, she was no stranger. The girl with the long, wild cloud of hair and the incredible figure had Del's small heart-shaped face, Del's velvety brown eyes and the cleft in Del's stubborn little chin.

Holy hell. He felt as if he'd been sucker punched right in the gut. Thank God he hadn't asked Peggy where Del was.

"Hey, Del," he said, making a superhuman effort to pull himself together and act normally. "Happy Birthday. Again."

"You missed the cake," someone said.

"That's all right." He was still looking at Del,

unable to process how his efficient vice president had become this…this hot.

And hot she most definitely was. Instead of her standard old baggy shirts, she was wearing that little black dress with spaghetti straps. She filled it out beautifully, and he was pretty sure it wasn't due to surgical enhancement, either.

"Nothing to say about Del's transformation?" Peggy asked. "The rest of us almost walked right past without recognizing her."

"I'd have done the same." He forced himself to tear his eyes away from Del. "It's a good thing she doesn't come to the office looking like that or we'd have clients crawling all over each other requesting a consultation with her."

The waitress approached then and he ordered a beer. Del got another drink, too, another of the green things in a big hurricane glass with a shamrock swizzle stick. But no one else did.

"Better not," said Sally from payroll. "I've got to drive and I need to get home to feed the dogs, anyway."

"My wife held dinner for me," the personal-security consultant said.

One by one, various people made their excuses and left until all that remained were Walker and his top-heavy date, Peggy, Del and him. After a few more moments, Peg also stood. "My youngest had a soccer game tonight. I figure I'll make it just in time to pick him up if I scamper now." She leaned down and bussed Del on the cheek. "See you Monday, birthday girl. Bye, boss, bye, Walker. Jennifer, it was nice to meet you."

"Oh, you, too." The redhead spoke with a breathy baby doll voice that sounded too silly to be real. It was the first thing she'd said since Sam had arrived, and he couldn't help turning incredulous eyes to Del.

When she met his gaze, there was amusement in the chocolate depths. He could almost hear her saying *Is she for real?* Suddenly he felt a lot more comfortable. She might have transformed her exterior but underneath she was still the person with whom he shared an almost uncanny nonverbal communication.

"Bye." Del spoke in unison with him. As Peggy maneuvered through the crowd toward the door, there was an awkward silence.

"So, Walker, we hired an assistant undercover consultant today." Del was quicker at making an effort to salvage the conversation than he was. "She's got a lot of experience with undercover work, which should complement Doug's capabilities." The undercover team typically assisted with bodyguard and surveillance work and often worked closely with Walker on abduction cases.

"A woman?"

Del nodded. "A very competent woman."

"Great," Walker said. "Since we got that little girl back from the relatives in France who stole her from the mother, we've gotten more work than Doug and I can comfortably handle. Someone with additional undercover expertise is just what we need. And it's probably a good idea to add a woman to the team."

"Oooh, you work undercover?" Jennifer turned on a high-voltage smile as she batted big blue eyes at Walker. She punched him playfully on the shoulder. "You didn't tell me that. How exciting!"

"Not really." Walker looked as if he was strangling in a tight necktie, except that he wasn't wearing one.

Sam took a closer look at Walker's date. Was she even legal? Beneath the boatload of makeup, the woman looked unbelievably young.

"What kind of work do you do, Jennifer?" Del stepped into the silence once again.

"Oh, I'm a model," she said. "Or at least, I wanna-be. Right now I take classes at the Barbizon School of Modeling and I work in the makeup department at Bloomie's."

A model wannabe? Jeez, there had to be a twenty-year age gap between Walker and his date. What the hell was the man trying to prove? Then Sam jumped as a small but lethal foot wearing a very pointy shoe kicked him in the shin. He turned and glared at Del but she was smiling at Jennifer.

"Modeling can be hard work." Del did her best to sound admiring.

"Uh-huh." Jennifer leaned forward. "I bet it's really fun being a secretary for these guys."

"Del's not a secretary," Walker said. "She's my boss."

"Wow!" The redhead clearly didn't know where to go with that statement. Eyeing Del critically, she said, "You know, if you're in management, you really should learn how to maximize your assets. I could fix you up with a makeover in no time flat. You'd be even more of a knockout with a push-up bra and—"

"Well," Walker said heartily. "Jennifer and I need to get going. Del, hope it was a good one. See you Monday, you guys." And with what was clearly the haste of a man in full retreat, he dragged his date out the door.

Sam watched them go. "Maximize your assets?"

Across the table, Del couldn't contain herself any longer. She snickered, then began to laugh. Her amusement was contagious and after a moment, he joined her.

"A makeover," she managed. "If she could only see my usual attire. She'd run screaming."

"It's probably past her bedtime," he said as their laughter subsided.

"Be nice." But Del's shoulders still were shaking with laughter. "What in the world is Walker thinking?"

Sam raised his eyebrows. "Do I really have to explain?"

"Besides the obvious," she said severely. "What could they possibly have in common?"

He only looked at her. "What else do they need?"

Even as the words hit the air, he realized the comment was a mistake. There was a moment of silence that, to him anyway, felt charged with erotic particles of sensual speculation. Though he'd often wondered about Del the woman, he'd never shared with her this kind of vivid awareness, a pull that made him want to reach over and set his mouth on hers.

Sam cleared his throat. "We seem to have been deserted," he said.

"The group doesn't usually stay late," she told him. "A drink, sometimes dinner and that's about it. Most everyone has a family to get home to." She twisted around and found the strap of her purse, which had been hanging on the back of her chair. "I appreciate you coming by, but don't feel you have to stay."

"I don't," he said, trying not to stare at the way her little dress shifted every time she moved. Suddenly, going home to his empty apartment seemed unbearable. "But I'm starving. I haven't eaten. Would you like to have another drink with me while I get a bite of supper?"

"Are you sure? This isn't just birthday pity?"

He felt the corners of his lips curving upward. "Nope. This is hunger speaking. I eat alone too much. Why don't you stay?" He shouldn't be encouraging her to linger. He was used to eating alone and the last thing he needed was for his vice president to think he was coming on to her. But he found he was waiting eagerly for her answer.

She hesitated a moment longer, then finally shrugged. "Sure. I don't have anything to rush home to."

"No pets?"

"Not even fish." She slanted him a wry look. "My boss is very demanding and I never know when I'm going to be needed for odd hours and overtime."

"Hey," he said, "you never said you minded. In fact, you often work harder and stay later than I do."

She shrugged again, making the little dress cling to her curves enticingly. One strap drooped off her shoulder and she impatiently hitched it back up. "Like I said, nothing to rush home to."

He had to concentrate to form a coherent answer. "Me, neither. I appreciate the company."

And he did. He was enjoying himself. While Del was efficient and not afraid to make her opinion known at the office, they rarely had time for personal exchanges. He'd learned more about her already tonight than he had in the past seven years.

"So why the transformation?" he asked. "You look great, but it's definitely a change from your usual garb."

"My mother sent this dress for my birthday," she told him. "Usually, the things she sends are so outrageous I wouldn't even wear them when I was alone. This wasn't too bad so I took a self-timed digital picture to send to her."

"Very thoughtful," he pronounced. "Why does she send you outrageous things?"

Del's eyes darkened as she took a sip of her drink. "Because that's exactly what she's like. Outrageous."

Two

"**I**'d like to meet her."

Del shook her head definitely, sending her hair slithering over her shoulders, and he was instantly distracted. What would it feel like to have that hair sliding all over *him?*

"Not in this lifetime," she said. She picked up her drink and took another long pull on the straw. "I only see her about once a year and trust me, that's more than enough."

There was the faintest note of bitterness in her tone. He wondered what her childhood had been like, to produce a reaction like that. If he asked her outright, she'd probably refuse to talk about it. So he went around the subject. "Do you have brothers or sisters?"

She shook her head again. "No, I'm an only. I was an accident."

"Your mother didn't want kids?"

"She was afraid they'd ruin her image."

Ah, so the woman was vain. Hard to imagine how she could have a daughter like Del, who purposely played down her looks. "And did you?"

She giggled. "No, but I certainly tried."

Had she just *giggled?* He couldn't believe it. There wasn't a woman on the planet less likely to utter a girly laugh than Del. "How much have you had to drink?"

"This is only my third," she said with great precision. "They're shamrock daiquiris and they're very good."

"Only your third? In a little while, those are going to hit you right between the eyes."

The waitress came by a moment later and he ordered a second beer and his meal. Del insisted on ordering another of her green concoctions, but he silently motioned the waitress to go light on the alcohol. Then he pointed to a small booth in the corner which had just emptied. "We're going to move back there."

He rose and grabbed his beer bottle.

Del stood as he rounded the table, picking up her drink and her bag. "Why are we moving?"

He pulled her chair back and took her elbow to guide her through the maze of tables. "That table's too big for just the two of us."

This close, he could see that the black dress was short. Very short. It exposed what looked like miles of long, slim leg. And she was taller than he was used to because she wore a pair of little strappy shoes with high heels.

Oh, man, he *loved* high heels on a woman with terrific legs. And Del did indeed have terrific legs. Long, muscled thighs, firm calves and slender ankles—he'd better get his mind off Del's legs before he embarrassed himself.

"Remind me," he said, "to thank your mother for this outfit sometime."

There was a moment of startled silence. Then Del said, "Do you like it?" She tilted her head back to peer at his face and almost lost her balance. "Whoops."

Sam put his arm around her waist—why hadn't he ever realized how delicate and slight she was?—and hauled her over to the table in the corner. He set her down on the seat. "Yeah," he said, hoping he hadn't overstepped the boundary between them. "I like it." *Like* was a vast understatement. The top clung to the curves of her breasts and dipped down to reveal the shadowed cleavage between them. All he wanted to do was lean down and place his mouth right there above the gentle swellings, to taste her fine-grained skin and feast on the scent that would be simmering there.

Telling himself that would be the stupidest move he'd ever make in his entire life didn't seem to help. But he forced himself to set down his beer and slide into the seat opposite hers. It was a snug fit for a man as big as he was. His legs tangled with Del's beneath the table.

"Sorry," she said, and she sounded breathless. "They must have decided to fill up this space with a downsized version of the real furniture."

He worked his legs around so that he could stretch them out on either side of hers. Not great, but bearable. Particularly when she moved and the outsides of her slim thighs brushed against the inside of his. Oh, yeah. Definitely bearable.

The waitress came by with his meal.

"Eat some fries," he said to Del.

"I already ate."

"Let me guess, a salad?"

She glared at him. "A *chef* salad, with ham. How did you know, anyway?"

"Because that's what you always get when we take clients out or order in." There. He might not have known her birthday but he did know something about her after all. "Eat some fries."

"You're just trying to keep me from getting too drunk," she accused.

"Yeah." He didn't see a reason to deny it.

"But I want to get drunk, Sam. I need to get drunk tonight if I'm going to meet a man."

He'd just taken a swig of beer and he damn near spit it out. "What? Who are you meeting?" He wasn't letting her meet anyone she didn't know really, really well in the condition she was in.

"No one in particular." Her voice was sulky. That was another first. Del in a mood. At work, she was quiet, reasonable, occasionally insistent and rarely annoyed. But the sexy little pout pushing out her full lower lip was one expression he'd never seen before.

"Are you telling me you're planning to pick up a guy in a bar tonight? No." He shoved his food away. "No, no, no."

"Whoa. Wait!" She grabbed the table and clung as he attempted to haul her to her feet. All that did was ensure that the table came with her as he started to drag her toward the door. "Sam, stop it! You're making a scene."

If there were any words he dreaded more, he couldn't imagine what they'd be. He let her go and straightened the table. Once she'd taken her seat, he also sat again, but he leaned across the small space, shaking a finger in her face. "You are not leaving this bar or any other with anyone besides me tonight. Got it?"

She blinked at the large finger waving beneath her nose. "That's a good way to get bitten," she said mildly.

"Wha—? Oh." He gave her his most menacing look although he was prudent enough to remove his finger from close proximity to her mouth first. "You're trying to change the subject."

"Yup." She nodded, leaning across to take one of his French fries. She nibbled it delicately and the motion of her soft pink lips made him swallow involuntarily.

"Why?" He didn't get it. "With all the scary stuff that can happen to a woman today, why would you take a chance like that, picking up a stranger?"

"It's very simple, Sam." She picked up her green drink and took a sip. "Do you know how old I am today?"

He shook his head. He'd honestly never thought about her age. She was just Del. "We started the company seven years ago," he said, thinking aloud.

"Right. And I was just out of college. Today I am twenty-nine years old."

"Congratulations?" He was mystified at her apparent annoyance.

"No!" She was glaring at him again. "I am twenty-nine years old and I've never had a boyfriend, much less a lover, in my whole life. I'm an old maid. And I refuse to let another year go by without finding out why sex is such a big deal."

She might as well have hit him over the head with a plank. "You're…you've never…"

"No." Her voice got softer and the animation drained from her features. "I've never."

"Why?" Why the hell would a woman who cleaned up as nicely as Del did still be a virgin at the age of twenty-nine? He was totally out of his depth. He heard the words and knew he needed to respond like a friend, but his body was responding as if he were a stud dog and a bitch in heat had just sashayed into his run. Ruthlessly, he shoved away the surge of desire that rose. "You're a beautiful woman, Del. I can't believe you've never had a guy interested in you."

She shot him a skeptical look, her finely arched eyebrows rising. "Don't be ridiculous. You know as well as I do my normal mode of clothing isn't exactly a man's fantasy."

"So? You could have found someone if you'd wanted." *I can't believe she's still a virgin!* "You hide your looks like some people hide their money."

"That's just it," she said. "I never wanted." She hesitated, then took a deep breath. "My mother was a party girl when she was younger. There were always men and booze and sometimes drugs around. She's been married several times since my father was killed when I was a toddler but not one of the marriages has lasted."

There was a wealth of pain in the simple explanation, and suddenly it was easier to think about something other than his own gratification. "Where were you when these parties were going on?"

"In my room. But I could hear. I used to sneak out when I was younger and watch sometimes. Then one evening a man found me and made some—" she made a disgusted face "—improper advances. My stepfather of the moment threw him out. When I got older, my mother was determined to marry me off. She started introducing me to potential husbands when I turned sixteen."

Sam realized his hands were clenched in tight fists on the tabletop and he made a conscious effort to relax them, taking a deep breath. "I begin to see why you dress the way you do."

She smiled grimly, gesturing at him with a French fry like a teacher with a pointer. "Exactly."

"So how did you escape?"

"Went to college on the other side of the country from my mother. And you know the rest. I came to work for you three weeks after graduation."

When he'd just been starting out. He remembered it well. He'd spoken of his new business to an acquaintance whom he'd met while he was convalescing. The man had told him he knew a young woman with a new degree in Business Administration who would be an asset. Gave her glowing references.

He couldn't even imagine the childhood she'd described. Visions of a poorly clothed child in a filthy room fending off her mother's drug-dealing friends troubled him. Why had he never known any of this about her before?

He knew exactly why, he thought as he scarfed down the sandwich he'd ordered. He wasn't the type of person to inspire confidences on the best of days. And Del, without the inhibition-lowering dose of alcohol she'd consumed tonight, wasn't the type to share them. He gave silent thanks to whatever god had led them to this juncture tonight. Clearly, he'd been put in Del's path to keep her from making a huge mistake.

"Del," he said carefully, "I can appreciate what you've told me. And I can understand it. But why now? If you've decided you're interested in a relationship, why not go about it in a more conventional way?"

"A relationship?" She made a sour face. "No. The last thing I want is some man trying to make me believe he loves me." She laughed, but there was little humor in it. "My mother was a shining example of matrimonial bliss. Thanks, but I'll pass."

"All right. So you don't want a relationship. But why pick up a strange man in a bar?"

She looked at him as if he were insane. "Where else do you suggest I go? Church?"

"Well, maybe, but there are other ways to meet guys."

"Such as?"

Damn. He couldn't think of a single thing except—"What about online dating services?"

She cast him a speaking glance. "Would you consider doing that?"

"Not a chance." Then he realized what he'd just said, and he narrowed his eyes. "That was a trick question."

He'd had plenty of occasions to become familiar with Del's stubborn streak over the years. When she didn't respond, he could tell from the mulish look on her face—the one he knew meant *You can say whatever you want but I'm still doing it my way*—that she wasn't going to listen.

"There's nothing wrong with being a virgin," he said desperately.

"Are you?"

"Of course not! But…that's not the point." His recovery time was a beat too slow.

"Why? Because you're a guy?" Suddenly there were tears in her eyes.

Oh, hell. Tears. He *hated* tears. In the seven years they'd worked together he'd never seen Del cry once. "No. Of course not. Just because…because…" He was drowning, going down for the third time without a life vest, and Del wasn't about to throw it to him.

All of a sudden she stood up. She slung her purse over her shoulder. "See? You can't come up with a single valid reason." And she turned and walked away.

Sam sat, distantly aware that his mouth was hanging open as he watched her totter toward the bar on those ridiculously high heels. Those high heels that did such wonderful things for her amazing legs. How crazy was it that this was the first time he'd ever seen those legs? No crazier than the conversation they'd just had, he decided.

Then he realized she was sliding onto a bar stool and he stood up. No way was he going to let her do something so final. He tossed a bill on the table which would cover their drinks and his dinner along with a generous tip, and strode through the throng toward Del.

"…work for a security firm. You know, like home alarm systems and things," she was saying to a very interested guy next to her as Sam got within range. Even half-toasted and undoubtedly pissed at him, he noted that she was suitably low-key when discussing the business. They'd agreed long ago that the best advertising for their unique services was word-of-mouth, that not everyone would appreciate the kinds of things they offered.

"Hey," said Sam.

She turned to face him, frowning. "Go away."

"I'd be happy to. And you're coming with me." In one smooth move he spun her stool around to face him and hefted her over his shoulder in a fireman's carry.

"Sam!" It was a half scream.

"Hey, buddy," said the guy beside whom she'd been sitting.

Sam shot him a single, bring-'em-on look, the kind he'd once used in combat. "She's with me."

The man put both palms up in surrender. "Okay, whatever, man. I was just making a little conversation. I didn't know…" His voice faded as Sam turned and headed out of the bar.

Del was wriggling and squirming and generally being a pain. For a moment he couldn't keep his hand from lingering over the firm curve of her bottom. The skirt was so short he could slide his hand beneath it in a heartbeat—*stop it, Sam!* "Settle down," he said to her. Her bare legs were smooth and muscled beneath his arm and he ran an appreciative hand down her calf as he let the outer door swing shut behind them. "Do you run or something?"

"I am going to *kill* you," she said in a muffled voice. Probably had a faceful of his shirt and her hair.

"Nah." He set her on her feet beside his car, trying to ignore the basic hunger that surged when she shook her hair back from her face with one of those unbelievably erotic little head tosses women did without thinking. "Tomorrow morning you'll be thanking me."

"I will *not*." He'd never seen her defiant before, either. She hugged her arms around herself as if she were cold, which she probably was in that skimpy outfit, and her voice quavered when she spoke again. "Tomorrow morning I'll be even more of a dried-up old prune than I am now. No man's ever going to want me." Her breath was hitching and by the time she finished, he could see in the glow from the streetlights overhead the shine of tears making tracks down her cheeks.

God, he hated it when women cried. There was nothing in life he hadn't been trained to overcome during his years in the Navy SEAL teams—except feminine tears. "Stop bawling, dammit!" Suddenly, he was completely out of patience with her, with himself, with this whole crazy evening. Why the hell was he staying away from her? He wanted her, had wanted her for…years, maybe. He'd just never let himself acknowledge it before. "You're not going to be a prune. If you're so damn determined to lose your virginity tonight, then it might as well be with me."

"You?" It was, to his ears, a horrified whisper.

"Me," he repeated grimly. "I'm clean, I'm nonviolent—unless called for—and I'm familiar. I'm good at sex. You'll like it." *And oh, baby, so will I.* "Now get in the car."

Quickly, before she could begin to argue, he put an arm around her and ushered her to the passenger side of his vehicle. "I'll bring you down to pick up your car tomorrow. You're not driving tonight."

He closed her door, rounded the hood and slid into the driver's seat of his Jeep Cherokee. Del hadn't moved, hadn't even put on her seat belt, so he leaned across her and snagged it, buckling her in. As he did, his forearm pressed against the soft, yielding swell of her breast. She made a small, panicked almost-sound and went perfectly still. His pulse raced and his body quickened, but he resisted the urge to devour her right there on the spot. For a few seconds, their faces were close together and he could smell the warm, woman scent of her, could feel her breath on his cheek, could hear the shallow gulps of air she was taking in.

"You okay?" he asked gruffly.

"No." She sniffed and another tear trickled down her cheek.

Sam lifted his hand and brushed it away with his

thumb. "Yes, you are," he said quietly. "Now let me take you home, babe."

She sat quietly while he started the car and headed out onto the Capital Beltway. He knew her address, though he'd never been there, and he needed little direction until the last few streets in her development.

"Turn left here. It's the third one on the right."

The third one on the right turned out to be a spacious town house with a bay window. It was built into a hill that fell away in the back so that she actually had three levels, he noted as he followed the curving street around to the parking area.

He helped Del out of the car and followed her closely as she went up the sidewalk. She still tottered a little on the heels and he wasn't sure if it was alcohol or simply lack of practice, but he put an arm around her waist, anyway, enjoying the feel of her slender body tucked against his side while she fished for her key in her handbag. *Soon,* he told himself, *soon you'll know everything there is to know about the body that's been hidden beneath those damn tents for all these years.*

When she came up with a small ring of keys and selected one, he took it from her hand. She looked up at him then and her eyes were dark, unreadable pools in the moonlight.

"Look, ah, Sam, I had a fair amount to drink and, ah, I mean—I know you were just kidding and I do appreciate you saving me from myself—"

"Why do you think I was kidding?"

She bit her lip. "You don't want me," she said in a small voice. "You're just trying to be nice."

He shook his head, stifling a strong urge to laugh at both her and himself. "I'm not nice." He debated with himself for a moment. What the hell. "And I do want you. I've wanted you for a long time."

Her eyes were huge as she absorbed the words. Suspiciously, she said, "You have? You're not just saying that to make me feel better?"

"I'm not just saying that."

"But why—"

"You're stalling." He put the key in the lock. "What was it you said? You weren't going to wake up tomorrow morning and still be a virgin." He opened the door, then turned to face her, taking her face between his hands and simply holding her there, examining her wide, wary eyes and trembling mouth. "You started it," he said, and his voice was rough with need, "you can finish it."

Three

He kissed her then. Holding her face cradled in his big hands, he set his lips on hers the way he'd imagined doing in countless idle daydreams. Daydreams he'd barely permitted himself to admit to having before tonight.

Her lips were soft and warm and she made a small noise as their mouths touched. Her hands came up and wrapped around his thick wrists and to his pleased surprise, she didn't fight him or passively accept. No, she kissed him back. Awkwardly at first, but she was definitely responding.

She's a virgin, he reminded himself. *Take it*

slow. And so he did, leisurely making love to her mouth alone, molding her lips with his until she was twisting and turning to meet him. He was dying to touch her, to slide his palms down her body and cup her soft bottom, to pull her up against his aching flesh until she could have no doubt about his interest in her. But he forced himself to keep his hands lightly on her face, concentrating on arousing her first. Slowly, he tasted her with his tongue, light flicking touches along the closed seam of her lips, and glory, hallelujah, she opened to him, inviting him in and even meeting him with shy tastes of her own. Her mouth was warm and sweet; she tasted of those green things she'd been drinking, and he pushed farther into the slick, moist depths, showing her what his body longed to do.

When he finally lifted his head, she sagged against him and her forehead dropped to rest against his broad chest. "You should be labeled 'explosive,'" she mumbled.

He grinned, dropping a kiss on the crown of her bent head as he let his hands fall to her bare shoulders beneath that glorious mane of hair. "May I come in?"

She lifted her head again at that, and her lips

looked swollen, glistening with his kisses. "I thought I didn't have a choice."

"You don't," he said, brushing his thumbs along the sides of her neck. She was like a drug—now that he'd finally begun to touch her, he wasn't sure he'd ever be able to stop. "I just wanted to make you feel better."

She snorted, though he noticed she didn't move away from his caressing hands. "What if I'd said no?"

"Then I'd have had to charm you with my irresistibility."

"That is not a word."

He was absurdly pleased to have his smart-mouthed, reliable Del back instead of the fragile, weeping woman he'd had in his car. "Wanna bet?"

She considered. "No."

He chuckled. He had never really thought about the easy working relationship they'd had. They'd been in sync from the very beginning, on the same page, often thinking the same thing at the same moment.

From the very first, Del hadn't been afraid to voice her opinion, to stand toe to toe and argue with him when she felt she was right. As she'd gained experience and knowledge, he'd had to concede to her more often. Hell, at least half the time her business sense was better than his.

They made a good team, he and she, he thought as he slid his hands from her shoulders down her back to her waist. He had the knowledge to offer their clients the specialized kinds of help they needed. Del had company management capabilities. They'd taught each other a lot, and their very different styles meshed well.

He knew at least half the employees were scared stiff of him. He wasn't terrific with people. *Okay, get real, Sam.* The truth was, he sucked at interpersonal stuff. He had no patience, no sense of finesse. He left that to Del. She was sympathetic, empathetic, all that "-etic" stuff, but she had a core of iron as well as a keen nose for bull and he'd bet on her in a verbal exchange of fire any day of the week.

Yes, they were a good match, playing little games like the one they just had.

And it had relaxed her. Her body wasn't tense and stiff against his anymore, but soft and pliant. He was the one with the stiff body now, he thought with grim amusement. And it was going to be a while until he wasn't anymore.

"Sam?" Del's head had settled on his shoulder,

her temple at mouth level. Without her shoes, he was pretty sure he could have rested his head atop hers.

"Yeah?"

"Can I ask you some questions?"

"Maybe," he said, "we should go inside and get comfortable."

"Okay."

For answer, he bent and slid an arm beneath her knees, the other around her back, and lifted her into his arms.

"Whoa!" She clutched at his neck. "What's with you carrying me tonight? Although I have to say this method beats the last one."

He stepped into her house and kicked the door shut behind him. There was a small nightlight of stained glass in shades of rose giving off just enough glow for him to get his bearings, and he headed for a couch along one wall. When he reached it, he pivoted and sank down with her in his lap. Not a bad arrangement, he thought to himself, tugging her closer as he yanked off his glasses and tossed them on her coffee table.

Then he remembered her words. "Okay. You wanted to ask me something?"

"Several somethings, actually." She took a deep breath that pressed her body against his and added fuel to the fire raging through his system. Her arms were still linked around his neck and he could feel her idly playing with the hair at his nape. It was an intimate, erotic action and his body responded immediately. And then her words sank in.

"Give me a break." He sat up straighter. "You were going to pick up a stranger and now you're *interviewing* me? I don't think so." Dropping his head, he sought her lips again.

Del was laughing but she quickly wound her arms around his neck, pressing her upper body against his as she opened her mouth and kissed him back. He plunged his tongue deep, seeking out the unique flavor that was Del. It seemed impossible that he really could be sitting here with her in his arms.

Not just in his arms, he thought. The rounded curve of her hip and bottom were pressed against the bulge behind his zipper, exciting him even more as the soft flesh yielded, cushioned his insistent arousal.

His free hand rested at her waist, and he spread his fingers wide, covering her flat belly. Slowly he smoothed his palm upward but before he reached the soft pillowed flesh he sought, he slid his hand back down and repeated the action, stopping just short of the swell of her breast each time.

Finally, she tore her mouth from his. "Touch me," she breathed. She took his wrist and urged it higher, and he breathed out a sigh of relief as the firm, soft mound of feminine bounty filled his hand. He shaped her breast with his fingers, then began to brush his thumb back and forth across the tiny bud of her nipple until it peaked and rose, the taut outline clearly visible through the thin fabric of the dress.

"It's time to get you out of this dress." He gathered her into his arms, then rose. She was surprisingly light, as he'd noticed before. He supposed he didn't think of Del as a small and delicate woman, but that's exactly what she was beneath all that businesslike competence. "Where's your bedroom?"

"Back down the hall on the left." She touched a finger to his bottom lip, tracing a light path around his mouth. "I didn't know a bed was required."

He strode back down the hallway and entered her bedroom. "For your first time, it's a damn good idea."

That sobered her and she took her hand away from his mouth.

"Hey," he said, "it's going to be all right."

She smiled but her lips quivered a little. "I know. I'm just…nervous."

Afraid, is what she meant. He imagined women

the world over felt very much the same way the first time they gave themselves to a man. And telling her it was going to be okay wasn't helping one little bit. He'd have to show her.

The room was dim and he didn't bother with the bedside lamp. There was enough light spilling in from the hallway as well as the moon that shone through her open curtains for him to be content, and he suspected Del would be more comfortable if it was dark, anyway.

He let her slide down to her feet beside the bed. Reaching for the hem of the little dress, he slowly tugged it up her body and over her head, tossing it carelessly into a corner.

Her hair was a loose, wild cloud spilling over her shoulders and he gently combed tresses aside, pushing them behind her shoulders until her torso was revealed. All she wore now was a lacy black strapless bra and a tiny pair of matching panties.

As he took in her slim, shapely figure, the generous slope of creamy breast and rounded hip, his palms nearly itched to touch her. "Del," he said softly. "I can't believe I let you hide from me all these years. What a dope I was."

She smiled again, a little less tentatively this

time. "I didn't exactly go out of my way to let you know I was interested."

"Were you? Interested?"

She nodded. "Very."

Very. She was right, she had hidden it well. If he'd had any idea a little alcohol would uncover the truth, he'd have taken her out for a drink a long time ago.

He slid his hands from her shoulders in toward her throat, circling her neck gently. Letting his thumbs brush downward, he skimmed the shadowed cleavage between her breasts and let his hand drop to the front clasp of her bra. It had been a long time, but he hadn't forgotten everything he knew, and he easily snapped open the simple fastening. The fabric sprang free but clung to her, caught on the peaks of her breasts, and he smiled as he slowly brushed over the satiny flesh and let the bra fall to the floor.

"Pretty," he murmured, bending his head. He set his mouth against her neck just below her left ear, kissing and tasting the tender flesh he found. "Very pretty." As his hands cupped the warm mounds, he lightly brushed his thumbs over their taut peaks, feeling them rise beneath his touch as he slid his mouth down the slender column of her throat to the delicate joining of neck and shoulder. He pulled her to him again then, turning her sideways and arching her backward over his arm as he bent his head to the breasts that jutted up at him. Lazily, he used his tongue to trace a wet circle around one brown tip, then lightly blew on the sensitive flesh, smiling when she shuddered. He flicked his tongue over her again, not missing the way she shifted restlessly in his arms, and then he couldn't wait any longer. Nuzzling his face against her, he took one nipple into his mouth, sucking gently at it, rolling his tongue smoothly around and around as he increased the suction. Her hands came up to clasp around his head and he felt her body relax. Become his. All his.

Gently, he eased her upright and knelt before her.

"What are you doing?" Her hands were rigid on his shoulders.

For answer, he tugged at the tiny panties, sliding them slowly down her smooth, bare legs. "We forgot these." It was an effort to resist leaning forward and burying his nose in the sweet, dark-curled cleft at the top of her thighs, but he reminded himself that Del wasn't used to such intimacy. So he stood, urging her toward the bed as he stripped off his shirt and kicked out of his shoes.

"Why don't we lie down?" If she were more experienced, vertical wouldn't be a problem. But he wanted her to be comfortable, to have wonderful memories of her first time. Her first time with him.

She began to slide onto the bed, but suddenly she stopped. "Aren't you going to undress?"

He nodded. "You can help," he told her, taking her hands and setting them at his belt buckle. He closed his eyes in delight as he felt her small hands fumbling with the belt, the tips of her fingers pressing against him as she found the zipper tab and slowly lowered it. She spread his pants wide and he said, "Ahhh," as his hardening shaft was freed from the tight strictures.

He looked down at himself. His stretchy briefs were…stretched, leaving little to the imagination. Putting his thumbs beneath the top elastic edge, he slowly pulled them out and down. As he freed himself completely and stepped out of the briefs, he wondered what she was thinking. Had she ever seen an aroused man before?

Just as he was about to reassure her that yes, it really would fit, Del said in a small voice, "May I…touch you?"

He smiled, trying not to look too much like the Big Bad Wolf in Grandmother's bed. "Sure."

But when she had permission, she hesitated. He reached for her hand and lifted it, slowly drawing her palm to him, wrapping her small fingers around him and holding her hand there with light pressure.

She looked up at him, eyes wide in the dim light. "It's soft!"

"No," he said definitely. "It is not."

"I know *that*," she said with a startled laugh. "I meant it feels velvety. Soft over hard." She explored a little, running her fingertips up and down and around, and he shuddered, feeling a dangerous frisson of pleasure slide down his spine. Hastily, he pulled her hand away with a rough laugh.

"I like that," he said, "but if you don't want this to be over right now, you'd better stop."

"I'm sorry," she said, perfectly serious.

"Me, too," he said with feeling.

He stepped around her and pulled the covers back to the foot of the bed. She slid onto the mattress while he donned protection, moving over as he followed her until she was on her back in the circle of his arm.

He gathered her close with one arm, the other resting at her waist. He was pressed against her soft hip, and if he'd ever known anything more erotic than this moment of sexual anticipation, he couldn't remember it. He kissed her gently, running his hands from her waist to her breast and down again. Letting himself sink into the flavor and scent of her, deepening the kiss until she attempted to turn more fully into his arms.

He slid his hand across her belly, stroking her soft skin, allowing his hand to trail lower with each movement until his fingers were stroking the soft, tight curls between her legs.

"What are you doing?" she whispered.

He knew she didn't mean it literally. "Taking it nice and slow," he told her. He eased one finger into her warm cleft. "Open your legs for me."

Her eyes were wide, searching his face, so he leaned down and kissed her again as he slipped his hand farther between her legs and found what he'd been hoping for. She was moist and slick, responding to his handling as if she'd been made for him. Probing deeper, he found her snug channel and inserted one finger.

She was tight. Very tight, and he felt sweat breaking out all over at the thought of what it was going to feel like when he was inside her. He'd better not think about that right now. "You okay?" he asked her.

She nodded. "It doesn't hurt."

He smiled tightly as he withdrew and returned, this time using two fingers.

She was breathing heavily, beginning to move restlessly against him. He smiled to himself as he bent his head and took her breast again. As he did, he slipped his fingers up through the dense nest of curls, searching out the tender bud hidden there. She gasped sharply as he pressed, then circled lightly, and her hips lifted off the bed. "Sam!"

"Del," he murmured against her skin. "Relax. Enjoy."

To his delight, she was amazingly responsive, her body reacting with every slight touch, every kiss, every breath she took. Her hands grew damp and frantic as she clutched at him, her nails digging into him as she tried in vain to pull him atop her.

He was having an increasingly difficult time keeping a lid on his own reactions. The feel of her satiny hip repeatedly pressing against him was a potent stimulant, and soon he found himself moving against her in response, pleasure shivering through his system with every subtle shift.

Finally, when he sensed she was as ready as she could be without completely sliding over the edge, he shifted his weight. Del accepted him eagerly, spreading her legs so that he could nestle himself in the warm cove of her thighs. Just the feel of her soft body beneath him threatened his control, and he quickly moved into position.

"This might not be comfortable," he warned her.

"I don't care." She urged him on, palming his buttocks and trying to pull him to her. "Please, Sam?"

He forced himself to move slowly, to enter her only one small fraction at a time before withdrawing and forging ahead a little more. Over and over again, he repeated the motion, his arms corded with the effort of holding back, every muscle in his body focused on the slick, tight glove of her body. She didn't seem to be in pain or even discomfort, her eyes shining and her warm body flowing around him. Suddenly, she arched her back, digging her heels into the bed and shoving herself up, offering him everything. The motion embedded him deeply within her, and he groaned as he felt his body slipping from his precarious control. His hips surged once, then again and again. He gritted his teeth. "Del," he ground out, "I-can't-wait."

"I can't, either," she panted. "Make love to me, Sam."

It was impossible to resist her plea. Letting his body take over, he ceased to think. Pure sensation reigned as he found his rhythm and urged her into following his lead, fiery pleasure spreading through him with each stroke. His body drew tighter and tighter as forerunners of ecstasy tap-danced down his spine. Del was moving wildly beneath him, with him, her slim body a beautiful sight.

She was making small sounds each time he moved against her, a whimpering, keening, needy sound that rose higher and higher until her body began to convulse beneath him, her tight sheath gripping him, milking him again and again as she shook and shattered. He couldn't wait, couldn't hold on, and with a rush of satisfaction he followed her, his body completing the mating ritual in the most primitive of ways, arching his spine and sending his seed forth in an explosive finish that nearly took off the top of his head.

In the aftermath, he slowly let his shaking arms relax and collapsed onto Del, burying his face in the pillow just beside her. Her arms came up around him immediately and the small motion created a warm glow deep inside him. She stroked his back lightly and as he moved to one side and drew her into his arms, he knew he was going to do his best to see that he spent a lot of nights from now on in Del's bed with her small body tucked securely against him.

Four

"**W**hy," he said, kissing the fragile shell of her ear that was mere inches from his mouth, "haven't we ever done this before?"

He felt her shoulder slide against his chest as she shrugged. "I always wanted you to notice me."

"I did notice you. I've spent countless hours over the past seven years wondering exactly what was under those huge shirts of yours." He cupped a breast in one big palm, gently brushing his thumb back and forth across the nipple. "Now I know," he said with deep satisfaction.

"You noticed me? Why didn't you ever do anything about it, then?" She ran her fingers through the hair across his breastbone.

He shrugged. "I'm shy?"

When she hooted with laughter, he tickled her until she screamed for mercy. Then she found the single tiny ticklish spot along the left side of his ribs and he was the one begging her to stop.

"I can think of some *s* words that describe you, but shy isn't one of them," she gasped, wiping tears of merriment from her face.

"Such as?" He smoothed her hair and settled her along his side again. He sandwiched one smooth thigh between his as she turned into his arms and nestled her head on his shoulder.

"Surly," she said.

"Me?" He was too preoccupied with his body's response to her to be offended. He was already half aroused again from their tussling and teasing, and her knee was lightly brushing some very sensitive territory. Having her sweet warmth so close and so very available was a form of the most pleasurable torture, because he knew she would be too tender, too sore, to accept him again that night.

"Everyone in the office trembles when you pass," she said.

"What happened to *s* words?"

"Scary," she said promptly, and laughed when he growled. "Sexy, of course."

"Of course."

"Smart, seductive, surprising depths—"

"That's two, but I like it."

He felt her smile against his skin. Then she gave a mighty yawn. "I'm sleepy."

"Go to sleep, then."

"Will you stay?"

"Yeah," he said. "I'll stay." *Just try getting rid of me, baby.* For some reason, he thought of her earlier question again. *Why didn't you ever do anything about it, then?* Why hadn't he ever thought about asking Del out? And then he knew. "You want to know why I never asked you out, Del?"

"Um-hmm." She sounded slightly more alert.

"Because I was afraid of what would happen when it ended. You'd have left and I couldn't have stood that. I need you, Del."

She stretched up and pressed a kiss against his chin. "I need you, too."

But she didn't. She had a life that could move on quite smoothly without him in it. But if she quit and he never saw her again… "I can't imagine running the business without you." It was inadequate, but he couldn't really express what he wanted to say.

Was it his imagination or did she shrink slightly away? He didn't move, but he pondered his last words. Did she think he hadn't paid her fairly for all the work she'd done through the years? He'd tried, but perhaps they should discuss it. Or maybe it was more than that—he'd wondered, on occasion, if he should make her a partner. He had no idea if she'd ever thought about it, had no idea if she had any capital to invest, but she deserved it. PSI wouldn't exist today if it weren't for Del, he was sure.

Then she said, "Lucky for you, you don't have to. 'Night."

He knew enough about women to know a dismissal when he heard one, so he shut up. Instead, he kissed her. To his immense relief, she lifted her face to his and responded, and he gathered her closer.

"Umm," she said. "What's that I feel?"

"Me appreciating you."

She laughed, and to his delighted surprise, slipped one small hand down between their bodies, exploring him with her fingers. "I didn't think men could, ah—"

"Some men can." He moved his hips, thrusting himself a little more firmly against her hand, groaning in pleasure when she gripped him firmly. "And would love to." He rolled to his back, spreading his legs slightly and giving her complete access to his body. "Wanna explore?"

She lifted her head and smiled at him, her eyes slitted with pleasure. "I'd love to."

The next morning, he awoke to an empty bed. The clock said it was after nine, and warm sunlight streamed into Del's tidy blue-and-white bedroom. He tossed back the covers and rose, stretching, then snagged his pants from the floor and headed for the bathroom.

Afterward, he followed the smell of coffee and bacon down to her kitchen.

She was sitting at the table, nursing a cup of coffee while she read the morning paper. Her hair was down, curling around her shoulders like a living curtain, and she wore only pajama bottoms and a brief camisole top that revealed the rounded shape of her breasts in a manner none of her daily work clothes ever had.

When their eyes met, heat flared and sizzled. But all she said was, "Good morning. Did you sleep well?"

Her tone was neutral. For a second he was puzzled—and then it hit him. She probably was embarrassed about last night—about the frank things she'd said and done—and she was expecting him to make quick excuses and leave this morning, having completed his duties last night. He sure as hell hoped that wasn't what she *wanted,* because he had no intention of going back to the unsatisfying way things had been before.

He was glad last night had happened. He was tired of being alone. It had been more than eight years since he'd been with a woman who meant anything more than simple relief, and he didn't realize how much he'd missed intimacy. Hadn't *allowed* himself to realize it, he supposed.

Crossing the kitchen, he scooped her out of her chair and sat down with her in his lap, settling her against his chest. He picked up her coffee cup and took a sip, then set it down and took a length of her unbound hair in his hand, gently stroking through it. "Good morning," he said. "I slept fine until I woke up alone."

"Sorry," she said, "I thought maybe you liked to sleep in on the weekends and I didn't want to disturb you."

"Not particularly. I'd rather spend time with you." Immediately he felt her body subtly relax, and triumph surged through him. He'd been right. "What do you want to do today?" he asked.

She shrugged, her camisole slipping lightly up and down against his bare chest. "I don't know."

"Well, what do you usually do on the weekends?"

Puffs of air blasted his chest as she chuckled. "Laundry."

He grimaced. "Me, too." Slowly, he slipped his hands beneath the hem of the little top she wore and ran his palms lightly up and down her back. She made a sound almost like a purr and relaxed even further in his embrace, and he gently cupped one of her pretty breasts, slowly rubbing his thumb back and forth over the sensitive tip that rose to meet him. He cleared his throat, but his voice was husky and deep when he spoke. "I've got some ideas on how we can spend the day."

Immediately, the tension returned to her body. "I don't think I can, at least until tonight," she said, regret in her tone. She pushed against his hold and rose from his lap, picking up her coffee cup and carrying it to the sink. "I'm sure you have things to do today and I actually do have a number of errands to run—"

"Whoa." He held up a hand, unable to believe his ears. Was she really giving him the brush-off because she thought all he wanted from her was sex? He rose and caught her hand, tugging her against him. "Del, I'd still like to be with you, even if we can't make love."

Doubt shone loud and clear in her skeptical gaze. "You would?"

"Yeah."

"Why?"

How in the world could a woman this appealing not have any idea of her own charm? He intended to find out more about her life until he figured it out. "As great as it was," he said gently, "I don't just want to jump your gorgeous bones. I want to spend time with *you*. Talking. Hanging out together."

She looked completely befuddled. "But if we can't—"

Sam put a hand over her mouth. Clearly, he wasn't getting through with words. He'd just have to show her. "After breakfast," he told her, "we'll go over to my place and grab my laundry. We can do it together and then maybe catch a movie or something later. Okay?"

She nodded solemnly behind his hand. "Okay."

He took a deep breath. "Would it be okay if I kept some clothes and things here?"

She looked at him as if he'd grown two heads. "What for?"

"So I can spend my free time with you," he said patiently, although her suspicious reaction put him on guard. He'd thought she would welcome the question.

She actually thought about it for a minute and he found himself actually breaking into a light sweat. Was she seriously thinking of refusing? "All right," she said at last. "I'll clear out a drawer for you if you like."

"I like." He tried to be as casual as she, although his brain was working overtime, picking apart the mystery that was Del. He'd expected his intent would signal his interest in establishing a more permanent relationship, that she would understand now that he meant her to be more than a handy bed partner. Instead, she'd nearly shot him down. He mentally added her reaction to the list of other questions he had in his head. Why would she be so skittish about letting him share her space?

And then he realized what he'd just been thinking. A permanent relationship. Holy hell, where had that come from? Yesterday he'd been happily single, today he was pondering the best way to get Del to let him move in. It was a pretty major shift of viewpoint, but he knew what had happened. For seven years he'd been watching Del without any real expectation of getting closer. But his subconscious knew what a prize she was, and the first moment that she gave him an opportunity, he'd recognized it.

And now that he'd gotten close, he had no intention of letting her push him away again.

Monday morning came too fast, in his opinion. The weekend had been unbelievable. Del was the most responsive woman he'd ever dreamed of, as she got past her initial inhibitions. He'd have been happy to spend another week making love to her. And he would, once her newly initiated body healed enough for more frequent lovemaking. Maybe, he thought wryly, if he kept her in bed that long he'd learn a little more about her. She'd said very little more about herself since the summary of her less-than-ideal childhood on Friday night.

"What's Del short for?" he asked as they were dressing for work.

"Nothing," she said.

"Just Del?" He was openly skeptical, although he knew from her personnel report that was the only name she'd used on any documents.

"Just Del," she said firmly. "Do you prefer Sam to Samuel?"

"Yeah." No point in explaining that Samuel wasn't the name he'd been given at birth. He'd been Sam for a lot of years and he liked it just fine. It still amazed him that no reporter had uncovered his legal name after the incident.

The Incident. That's how he'd come to think of it in the years since, that stupid little label the media often used to describe horrific events.

"Are you ready?" Her question jarred him from his unwelcome introspection as she picked up her briefcase and headed for the door.

"Right behind you."

They'd picked up her car from O'Flaherty's on Saturday, but he saw no sense in them driving separately to work now. He had every intention of coming home with her again tonight. Still, once they reached the office, Del insisted on entering individually.

"Why?" The way she kept trying to keep him an arm's length away was beginning to rankle.

She shrugged. "I'd rather the entire company didn't know we have a personal relationship now."

He hooted at her prim tone. "You mean you don't want them to know we're sleeping together."

She glared at him. "Well, yes. Hasn't it occurred to you, in this age of sexual-harassment suits, that it might not be such a great thing to broadcast?"

He sighed. "Del. We both know there's no harassment involved—unless the fingernail marks you left on my behind last night count—and we're the only ones who matter."

She blushed to the roots of her hair. Finally, she smiled and a wash of relief rolled through him. "Okay. But would you just humor me? I already feel like I'm wearing a sign that says, 'Sam and I…'"

"Are doing the mattress dance?" he suggested, laughing.

"Ick!" She punched his shoulder, then reached for her door handle. "Just like a man. If you're going to be crude, I'm outta here."

"Hey." He caught her hand as she began to slide out of the car."

"Hmm?" She turned to face him.

He leaned across the seat and claimed her mouth in a brief, stirring kiss. Her lips softened and warmed beneath his before he drew away. "Thanks for this weekend."

She smiled softly, touching his cheek with a gentle finger. "I'm the one who should be thanking you."

He gave her a head start, then casually entered behind her. He paused in the outer office where Peggy reigned. She and Del already were bent over some forms on Peg's desk. "'Morning, Peg. 'Morning, Del."

"Hey, boss." Peggy glanced up at him and her eyes widened. She immediately fastened her gaze on Del. "Yee-haw!" she hooted.

"What?" Del jumped and lifted her head.

"It's about time you two got together," Peggy said.

"What makes you think we did?" Del asked.

Peggy grinned. "You're glowing and he smiled at me."

He raised his eyebrows and tried to look fierce. "And that's a sign of…?"

"Sam," said Peggy. "You *never* smile before you've had your coffee. Besides, Del's blushing."

Oh, hell. Now they were going to be the water-cooler topic of the week. He quickly escaped to his inner sanctum, leaving Del to fend off Peggy. Women were better at that kind of thing, anyway. As he closed the door, though, he heard Peggy say, "The air around you two has been sizzlin' for years. If I'd have wet my finger and stuck it between you I'd have gotten electrocuted."

Had he been that obvious? Interesting that Peggy had recognized it before he had.

At nine, Karen Munson came in to fill out more paperwork and meet the people with whom she'd be working. Since the undercover-division leader was on vacation until Friday, Del had arranged to have Walker show her the ropes and bring her up to speed on current contracts. Walker was the head of the abductions division, but he often worked closely with undercover so it wouldn't be much of a stretch.

That was fine with Sam, since he needed Del to help him work up an estimate for a new job they'd just gotten. Karen was in Del's office so when he heard Del page Walker, he got up and went to the door that led from his office to Del's.

He walked across the room with his hand extended. "Good to have you on board," he told Karen.

"Thank you." She didn't quite smile, but the serious expression that seemed to be her norm lightened a little. "I'm looking forward to getting started."

A knock on the door preceded Walker's entry.

"Come on in," Sam called. To Karen, he said, "The head of our abductions team is going to explain our procedures to you and bring you up to speed on our current contracts. Undercover employees often work closely with abductions and surveillance."

As Walker entered the room, Sam turned to him, indicating the new hire. "Walker, I'd like you to meet—"

"Karen!" Walker's shocked exclamation echoed through the room. "What the hell are you doing here?" He made the question an insult.

"I'm working here now," she said coolly, although she looked nearly as shaken as Walker was, "as you apparently do."

"No way." Walker's eyes narrowed. "This work isn't going to suit you."

"You have no idea what suits me anymore," she said sharply.

"Did she tell you she's my wife?" Walker demanded, wheeling to face Sam. His big hands were actually fisted at his sides.

"Ex-wife." Karen's tone was frosty. "And no, amazingly enough, your name never even entered the conversation during my interview. I had no idea you worked here." *Or I'd never have taken the job.* The unspoken words hung in the air like glass slivers in a broken window's frame.

"I can't work with her." Walker wheeled and stalked to the window.

Sam looked at Del, silently questioning her with his eyes. *What the hell do we do now?*

Del's eyes were the size of saucers, but as always, she rose to the occasion. "Sam, why don't you and Walker go into your office?" she said. She indicated the door to the hallway as she turned to Karen. "I'll take Karen down to her desk and get her started."

As she led Karen from the room, she glanced back at him, and he read her response. *Calm him down!*

Great. She got the lamb and he got the lion. Pushing a hand through his hair, he said, "Walker. My office." He turned without waiting for a response and entered his own office again, taking a seat behind his desk. Intuition told him authority was going to be important right now, though he'd always had an easy, friendly relationship with the bigger man in the past.

Walker followed him in, every muscle in his solid frame looking tense and taut. "I mean it, Sam," he said in a deep, furious tone. "I can't work with that b—"

"Hey," Sam said. "Walker. Chill. Take a deep breath." He took his own advice, watching Walker pace around the perimeter of the room. "I didn't know." Honesty compelled him to add, "But I might have hired her anyway. She's exactly what we're looking for."

Walker spun around and glared at him. "She's *not* what we're looking for. We need a dedicated individual who can be as flexible as we need her to be. Karen doesn't know the meaning of the word." His tone was bitter. "It's her way or no way."

"She says she'll work as long and as hard as we need her to." Sam watched his abductions expert closely, wondering what had gone wrong between the couple to make Walker still feel this way after so many years. Karen Munson must have been the woman responsible for the binge Walker had gone on that time he'd come in so hungover, but Walker had indicated then that the marriage had been over some years before he'd come to PSI.

"She's got a family," Walker said harshly. The words sounded raw and accusatory. "She's always going to put her husband and kid above the job."

Sam cleared his throat. Karen Munson hadn't stipulated that the information she'd shared with him was private. Quietly, he said, "Her child is…deceased."

Walker's angry gaze flew to his, incredulity replacing the rage. *"What?"* It was an explosion.

Sam just watched him.

"God." Walker dropped heavily into a chair and buried his head in his hands as his anger visibly drained away. "Is she still married?" he asked in a muffled tone.

Sam could answer that. After the initial interview, he'd checked out Karen's application. "She listed herself as a widow."

Walker raised his head and there was more anguish in his gaze than Sam had seen in anyone's eyes since he'd woken in a hospital bed and his commander on the teams had had the unenviable task of telling Sam he'd probably never walk again. "They're both dead?" he whispered.

"You knew she was married and had a child?"

The other man nodded. "That's why she left me. I wasn't willing to settle down." Remembered agony twisted his features. "She replaced me faster than you can say 'I do.'" He heaved a deep sigh. "God, I've hated her for years. But I never wished anything like this on her. What happened?"

Sam shrugged. "She didn't get into it. Just made us aware that she was free to work pretty much anytime we needed her."

"I don't think I can work with her." Walker sounded defeated.

"Why don't you—"

But the other man shook his head. "She cut out my heart, Sam. I just don't think I can do it." Slowly he rose to his feet, walking toward the door like a man much older than forty. "My resignation will be on your desk by the end of the day."

"I won't accept it."

Walker turned, his hand on the doorknob. "You'll have to."

But Sam shook his head. "You're the best at what you do, buddy. I'll tell Karen we can't employ her."

Walker stared at him a moment. "You can't do that."

"Wanna bet? I'm not about to lose you."

There was a taut moment of silence, humming with tension.

"Damn." Walker's shoulders slumped. "You know I wouldn't do that to her. Especially now, after…"

"I was hoping so." Sam got up from behind his desk and walked across the room to the man who'd been one of his first hires and most faithful employees. "We'll look at the structure and see if we can't work something out so you don't have to work closely together, all right?"

He held out his hand. After a moment, Walker took it and they shook. "I'd appreciate it," the big man said quietly, and left the room.

Five

An hour later, he heard Del return to her office. Moments after that, she came through the connecting door. "Hey," she said.

"Hey."

"I got Karen settled, showed her around. She's reading over the current workload for the rest of the day." She perched on the corner of his desk and blew out a deep breath. "What a bombshell."

He took off his glasses and massaged the bridge of his nose. "I sure wasn't expecting that."

She grimaced. "I had no idea they'd been married."

"I looked at her file again. It's not mentioned in there but there isn't any reason it should have been."

She picked up his glasses and fiddled with them idly. "What are we going to do?"

He shrugged. "Nothing. We hired her. Walker's going to have to deal with it if he stays. I can't just fire her because he doesn't want to work with her." He paused. "I told him we'd try to figure out something so he didn't have to work with her much."

A single elegant eyebrow rose. "You think we can manage that?"

"To some extent."

"I guess you're right." Del started cleaning his glasses with the tail of her shirt. Then she held them up to the light. A moment later, she lowered them and looked at him with a strange expression. "Sam?"

"Yeah?" He was still thinking about Walker's defeated expression. He'd felt like that for a while after Ilsa had dumped him. He never wanted to feel it again, either.

"Why do you wear glasses if you don't need them? These aren't prescription lenses, are they?"

Hell. He'd completely forgotten about that. "No," he said slowly, "they aren't."

"So why do you wear them?" she asked again.

He searched for an explanation she would accept. *Because I don't want to be recognized* was definitely not the right one. "I've found they make people take me more seriously." That was lame.

But Del's face lit up with amusement. "You mean women, don't you? Poor baby. Were you getting hit on a lot?"

He narrowed his eyes. "You think that's funny?"

"I think it's true." She was laughing. "Sam Deering. Hunk of the year."

She had no idea how accurate that was and because she didn't, he was able to laugh. He shot out a hand and grabbed her elbow, yanking her off her perch on the edge of the desk and into his arms. "So you wanna hit on me?"

She slipped her arms around his neck, running her fingers through the curling hair that lapped over the collar of his denim shirt in the back. "I might."

He lowered his mouth to hers. "Notice me struggling."

"Hey, boss, I've got—Whoops!" Peggy barged into the office and just as quickly retreated, shutting the door behind her. From the other side of the closed door, they could hear hoots of laughter.

"Damn," he said, regretfully releasing Del. "There goes my office credibility."

"What about mine?" Del straightened her shirt, blushing furiously.

"You don't have to worry. I'm irresistible, remember?"

She groaned. "Not that again." But she was laughing as she went to open the door for Peggy.

Other than that Monday-morning explosion with Walker and his ex-wife, it was the best week of his life. He and Del arose together, ate breakfast together, went to work together in the morning. At work, after the time Peggy had caught them on Monday, they were the model of propriety except for the occasional blood-pressure-raising exchange of glances.

Until they were alone together after everyone else had left the building.

Then he couldn't seem to keep his hands off her. It didn't prevent their work from getting done if he pulled her into his lap while they argued the cost estimates on a project. And it didn't slow them down too drastically if, while she was showing him the layout for the new brochure, he slipped his hand up beneath her baggy shirt and cupped one rounded breast, teasing the nipple into stiff attention until her eyes clouded and she pulled away.

"Stop," she said. "I can't think straight when you do that."

Good. He didn't want her to think straight. He wanted her to think Sam. Only Sam.

After work they prepared meals together. Del was no better and no worse than he was in the kitchen. Between them they could put together a decent stuffed chicken, potatoes and a salad.

It amazed him, when he stopped to think about it, how easily they'd fit into each other's lives. It was as if they'd been together for years. Which, he supposed, wasn't far from the truth. While they hadn't lived together, they'd worked so closely together that they knew each other's quirks and moods without speaking.

He knew her favorite kind of pizza—pepperoni—and that when she was annoyed her eyes became as green as emeralds. She knew that ice cream gave him indigestion, and that he couldn't knot his tie to save his life. Her habit of drumming her fingers on the table while she was thinking aggravated him endlessly, and when he chewed on the end of practically every pen he picked up, she fussed at him about spreading his germs to everyone in the company.

But in many ways, she was still an enigma. As

far as he could tell, her life was as solitary as his. She didn't appear to have any close girlfriends, and the calendar on the wall in her kitchen was conspicuously empty, except for a few notations about birthdays for co-workers. It appeared that her life revolved around PSI as much as his did.

That was weird. Most women were nesters in one way or another, drawing at least one or two people close even if they weren't highly social. He'd never heard Del speak of a single person who wasn't connected with the company other than her mother. And though she was close to several of the other PSI employees, particularly Peggy, he'd noticed the relationships seemed largely to end at the office door. *Except for birthday parties,* he thought, smiling to himself.

Friday evening, they took a prospective client to dinner, a West Coast actress who had been receiving death threats. Sam always invited Del along to meet prospective clients, and she usually attended. She was so much better than Sam at putting people at ease that he found her presence a welcome buffer.

As they were getting ready to go out, Del said, "Tell me again why Savannah Raines wants to hire us?"

Sam glanced across the bedroom. "Stalker," he said briefly. Then he stopped in the act of donning his charcoal suit coat. "You're wearing that?"

"That" was a shapeless black pantsuit. Now that he thought about it, he realized Del had worn the exact same outfit to every dinner meeting they'd had over the past seven years.

She glanced down at the boxy black jacket and equally loose black slacks. "Yes. Why?"

Sam walked across the room, thinking about the best way to word his objections. "You've worn it a lot before."

"So?" She was looking at him in bewilderment. "It's comfortable."

"It helps you hide, is what you mean," he said.

"Hide?" Her voice was chilly, but he didn't care. Someone, somewhere, had given Del reason to believe she wasn't attractive, and Del had been playing down her every asset ever since, he'd bet. "You hide behind glasses with useless lenses."

"You're a beautiful woman," he said, ignoring her words as he crossed to her. "That dress your mother sent you looked terrific on you the other night. This—" he indicated her unflattering suit "—is like everything else you own—designed to make you invisible."

"Maybe," she said stiffly, "that's what I'm aiming for. Maybe I like being invisible."

"Do you?"

She hesitated, and he realized she hadn't expected him to challenge her aggressive words. "Most of the time, yes," she finally said. "I have good reasons for not wanting to attract attention." Then she smiled, and he felt himself responding to the sensuality in her knowing gaze. "But I'm glad I wasn't invisible last Friday night."

"Me, too," he said, meaning it. He was willing to let the subject drop for the time being, but he knew she thought she'd successfully sidetracked him. If she thought he was going to forget about it, she didn't know him very well. She'd really piqued his interest with that simple statement: *I have good reasons for not wanting to attract attention.* What reasons could be good enough to make a woman work that hard to hide her natural beauty?

Savannah Raines's husband came with her, and over dinner they discussed her best options for keeping herself and her family safe as well as for locating the individual making the threats.

The actress was surprisingly pleasant and

down-to-earth and her husband, an architect, was nothing like some of the idiotic Hollywood types they occasionally dealt with. Sam would have enjoyed the meal except that Del was being almost monosyllabic. She wasn't rude or unfriendly, in fact she was better than he at explaining what PSI could do for Savannah. But when they weren't talking business, she sat back and seemed more than content to let him hold up the conversation, which was definitely not his strong suit. Usually, it was hers, and he wondered if she wasn't feeling well or something.

He glanced at her, sitting quietly in the corner of the booth beside him just as Savannah said to Del, "You know, dear, you look so familiar to me. Have we met somewhere?"

Del raised one eyebrow, a unique trait that always intrigued him. "I doubt it, Ms. Raines. Have you been to Virginia before?"

The question implied that Del was a Virginia girl, and Sam knew for a fact that wasn't true. She'd graduated with honors from Williams College, an exceptionally selective liberal-arts school in Massachusetts, shortly before he'd hired her. It suddenly dawned on him that he had no idea where she'd lived before that, and he cast her a sharp look. How was it they'd worked together so long and he knew so little about her formative years? He deliberately stayed quiet about his own past because he had something to hide. But it seemed that so did she: *I have good reasons for not wanting to attract attention.* The sentence kept replaying in his head.

What reason could Del possibly have for her reticence? What was she hiding? Somehow, he doubted it was anything as earthshaking as his desire not to have half the country recognize him when he walked out his front door.

At the end of the evening, they said goodbye to their guests and Sam helped Del into the front seat of his Jeep. He hadn't forgotten his thoughts from earlier in the evening.

As they drove back toward her place, he said, "You lied by omission in there tonight."

"What?" Del sounded understandably bewildered.

"You let Savannah believe you grew up in Virginia. Did you?"

"No." Her bewilderment acquired a distinct edge of irritation. "I just didn't see any point in going into my background."

"Guess where I grew up." He knew she'd get pricklier if he pressed her, and though he was determined to get some information out of her tonight, he was prepared to take his time and go about it leisurely.

She paused, apparently searching her memory banks. Finally, with an air of surprise, she said, "I don't know. California?"

The guess was incorrect, but it shook him. He'd never told anyone at the company that he'd been based in San Diego during his years with the teams. In fact, he didn't think anyone even knew he'd been a SEAL. They knew he was ex-military but he knew most of them assumed he'd come from the army and he'd never done anything to correct their impressions.

"No," he said in answer to her guess. "I lived in California before I started the company. But I grew up in Nebraska."

"Nebraska?"

He glanced across the car and was amused to see that single eyebrow raised again. "Yep. On a ranch a few miles from the South Dakota border."

"You're kidding. I never would have pegged you for a cowboy."

He grinned. "I hide it well."

"You can ride a horse?" She sounded highly skeptical.

"Of course I can ride a horse. On a ranch, everybody rides. I learned to drive when I was thirteen, though, because my dad got thrown and broke a leg that summer."

"I didn't learn to drive until I was in college," she said.

"Why?" He was startled. That was far more unusual than learning to drive early.

She shrugged. "Never really needed to before that. Are your parents still in Nebraska?"

He nodded, aware that once again she'd neatly avoided talking about herself. "And my younger brother and sister. David and his wife have three sons and they live in the house where I grew up. My sister, Rachel, lives about twenty minutes away with her family. Mom and Dad moved into a smaller house on the property a few years ago."

"So you're the only one who moved away."

"Yeah." He took a deep breath. "I joined the navy."

This time she turned fully in her seat to stare at him. "You're full of surprises tonight. I thought you were army."

"Nope."

"Why the navy?"

"I wanted to be a SEAL."

She was silent for a moment. Finally, she said, "That explains it."

"Explains what?"

"The way you seem to know everything there is to know about the weird military stuff."

He was amused again. "Weird military stuff. Such as?"

"Such as every kind of explosive on the market, weapons I've never even heard of, the best ways to get people in and out of places they shouldn't be in the first place." She took a breath. "You always consider the worst-case scenario and plan for it. That's one of the reasons we're so successful. When we take on a job, it gets done even when something unexpected forces us to alter the original plan."

He didn't quite know how to respond to that. He'd never really thought about it before. "Building this company has been exciting," he said, "but we never would have become what we are today without you. I'd better remember to thank Robert someday for recommending you."

"How did you meet Robert?" she asked.

Yikes. He wasn't quite ready to go there yet, although he supposed that someday he would have to tell Del about his past.

"A year or so before I started PSI, I had an injury that ended my navy service," he said. It was true enough; he just didn't mention how he'd been hurt. "I was trying to decide what I was going to do with my life. So there I was, lying on a gurney in the hospital waiting for some X rays and this guy starts to talk to me. He was there for knee surgery and we both had to kill some time until they came for us. Turned out he once was married to an actress—he had all kinds of advice for me about how to avoid losing my privacy."

"Robert." Her voice was quiet. She'd become very still while he'd been speaking and he wondered what she was thinking.

"Yes," he said. "So how did you know him? When he recommended you, I got the impression he'd known you for a long time."

"He was a family friend."

"A friend of your mother's?"

"Um-hmm."

"He's a great guy." And Sam couldn't imagine the distinguished, elegant Robert hooking up with the woman Del had described. But who knew?

"Were you injured during a mission, or whatever you call it?"

The question caught him off guard, though he

supposed he should have expected it. She'd seen the bullet wounds the first night they'd made love. The one that had ripped through his bicep didn't look too bad.

But the other one told a different story. The slug had entered just above his left hipbone and torn its way through his body to exit through his back. It had nicked his spine and though he'd lost bits and pieces of several organs, that hadn't been the damage that worried his doctors the most. He'd experienced temporary paralysis. Of course, no one had known it was temporary until it began to fade, and he'd spent weeks adjusting to the thought of life as a paraplegic.

And as a man who'd been dumped when he was no longer the able-bodied SEAL his fiancée had wanted.

He still could barely stand to think about those days. But she needed an answer.

"Sort of," he said briefly, hoping she wouldn't pursue the topic.

"Your injuries look as if they were serious."

"They were." He didn't have to dissemble about that.

There was a moment of silence. He didn't look at Del, but he could feel her gaze measuring him. Finally she said, "I'm glad you didn't die."

They had arrived, and he pulled into the parking lot and cut the engine before responding. Then he reached for her in the dark interior of the vehicle, hauling her into his arms. Just before he took her mouth, he said, "I'm glad I didn't die, too. I'd never have met you."

She kissed him back with all the fire and passion he'd come to expect, but when he lifted his head, she didn't say anything more.

"Shall we go in?" he asked.

She nodded. "Let's."

As they started up the steps together, it occurred to him that they had never had any kind of conversation that hinted at future plans. She'd reluctantly agreed to let him bring over some of his things, and throughout the week he'd gradually brought more and more, until he had enough changes of clothes that he didn't have to go home for a week if he didn't want to. She had to have noticed, but she hadn't protested, and he'd taken that as a good sign.

But sudden uncertainty pulled him to a halt in the hallway just outside her door. "Del?"

She glanced up at him, smiling as she extracted

her key from the purse she'd carried this evening in a departure from her usual backpack. "Hmm?"

"Are you okay with this? With us?"

The door swung open, but she continued to look at him. "Yes. Are you?"

She'd answered him, so he didn't know why he felt unsatisfied. Maybe he hadn't asked the right question. "Yeah," he said. "I am."

But something within him wanted more. More what, he wasn't sure. But he definitely wanted more from Del and he wasn't at all sure she was prepared to give it.

That night, for the first time in more than six months, he had the dream.

He was walking down a street not far from the utilitarian apartment in San Diego where he lived when he wasn't on an op. He was carrying a sack of groceries he'd picked up at the corner store.

It was a sunny Saturday afternoon in November and the temperature was shirtsleeves pleasant. There were tourists crowding the seafood market and checking out the little boutiques that had overtaken the rougher elements of the neighborhood a few years ago. It was a perfect day.

And then a madman opened fire.

He instantly recognized the rapid, distinctive sound of shots and reacted. But as he went rolling for the dubious cover of a nearby parked car, he felt a punch in his left shoulder, followed moments later by a searing pain.

He'd been shot!

And whoever had done it was still shooting.

Dammit. In his years with the navy, he'd never suffered more than cuts and bruises and once, a concussion from a blast that had gone off a little too close for comfort. And here he was, at home on leave with a bullet wound in his shoulder. God must enjoy a good joke.

Cautiously, he peeked around the fender of the car. A lone man was strolling down the street at an almost leisurely pace, about twenty-five yards away. Three people lay sprawled on the pavement behind him, unmoving. At least one, a man, was clearly dead, Sam was sure, from the awkward angle at which the body had fallen. Another woman knelt on the pavement not far from where the guy was walking, a child cradled in her lap.

The shooter raised his pistol and shot her through the head.

Sam recoiled, his brain rejecting what he'd just

seen. He heard another shot, a piercing scream and then another shot. The screaming stopped instantly.

God, this guy was executing people! Instantly, his mind went into what he privately thought of as protection mode, automatically seeking and assessing his chances of eliminating the enemy while saving his own hide and those of all the other people around him.

He glanced behind him, down the street in the other direction. Several people lay where they'd fallen when they'd been hit. Most of them were moving. And Sam would bet there were more people who'd taken cover just like him. This could be a massacre of devastating proportions.

In a doorway opposite him, a woman in a shopkeeper's apron crouched, her eyes wide and terrified. A kid in the baggy pants and backward ball cap of a teenager lay a few feet from her, blood staining his pant leg and the pavement beneath him. He was trying to drag himself to the shelter of the shop's doorway.

Sam could hear the gunman's footsteps approaching.

"Hey, buddy," the guy called to the bleeding kid. "What'samatter? You afraid?" He laughed, a chilling cackle that Sam would hear in his head for the rest of his life. "Lotsa people gonna die today," he said in a singsong voice.

Sam gathered himself, every muscle in his body quivering, raring for action. The guy wasn't close enough for a grab; he was going to have to sprint to get to him. And if he wasn't careful and accurate—and fast—the woman and the injured boy would die next.

The gunman took a few more steps. This was as good as it was going to get.

Sam launched himself from behind the car, directly at the man with the gun.

The guy turned at the sound of Sam's footsteps but by the time he'd swung his gun around, Sam was on him. Both men went tumbling to the pavement, elbows and heads striking the unforgiving surface as they fell. Another shot rang out and Sam felt a tremendous kick in the region of his left kidney. As he wrestled with the insane killer, a small part of him registered that he'd been shot again. But no pain. Not yet. He didn't have time to worry about it as he struggled to immobilize the man before he could kill anyone else.

The guy still had a death grip on the gun and he was shooting wildly. There were so many people around he was almost guaranteed to kill some-

one else…. In a split-second decision, Sam did what he'd been trained to do. With one powerful arch of his body, he broke the gunman's neck.

The silence was shocking after the noise of the weapon.

Sam lay where he was, the killer's limp figure half atop him. As his concentration receded, he began to hear sounds. Sirens, people sobbing, several people moaning and screaming. The kid nearby was softly crying for his mother.

The woman who'd been crouching in the doorway ran to the boy's side. "Lie still," she said. "You're going to be okay."

"I'm a nurse," shouted an unfamiliar voice as footsteps ran toward him. "We need to identify all the wounded and prioritize them by who's most critical."

The shopkeeper said, "I can put pressure on this boy's leg. He didn't hit a major blood vessel. But that guy over there—the one who stopped him— he might need help. He got shot when they were fighting."

The footsteps came closer. He shoved at the gunman's dead weight, rolling the body ignominiously to one side in a careless heap. The movement sent a nauseating wave of red-hot pain ripping through his abdomen, rippling out to every cell in him.

Gritting his teeth against the agony, he raised his head and looked down at himself. The second bullet had hit him in the lower left torso. Blood darkened his shirt and his jeans and was beginning to pool on the sidewalk around him.

He tried to gather himself, but his legs weren't cooperating. The woman who'd said she was a nurse knelt at his side. "Hang in there," she said. "Help's on the way."

And it was. Sam could hear the sirens drawing to a screaming halt, doors slamming and gurneys clattering as medics rushed toward the injured.

"This one first," his comforter yelled.

Sam caught her eye. "That bad, huh?" It came out a hoarse whisper.

She shrugged, but she met his eyes and he saw the truth there. "Not so good," she said, "but you can't die on us, you're a hero."

Six

Two weeks later, they had settled into a comfortable routine. Since the night they'd made love for the first time, they had been together nearly every minute. They worked together and then came home, usually to her place, together. They ate together and slept together, although neither one of them was getting nearly as much sleep as they needed. Sam had gradually moved darn near every important piece of clothing he owned—as well as a few books and all his toiletries—into her apartment.

They were sitting on the couch watching television on a Sunday evening when he finally decided to get it over with. He'd been wanting to talk to her all weekend about their living arrangements and had been putting it off like a big sissy.

"Del?"

He had his arm around her and she lazily turned her head against his shoulder until she could see his face. "What?"

"Do you like it here?"

He got The Eyebrow. "Here, as in Northern Virginia, or here as in on this couch this very minute?"

Trust Del to pick apart the semantics.

"Here as in this town house," he said.

"Well, yeah, or I wouldn't be living here." She sat up and looked at him questioningly. There seemed to be a hint of suspicion in her voice, or maybe that was just his own paranoia kicking in. "Why?"

He shrugged. "We seem to be spending all our time away from work together, and it seems kind of a waste to have two places to live." He stopped and held his breath.

She searched his eyes. "You mean you want me to move in with you?" She sounded sincerely stunned.

"Or I could move in with you," he said hastily.

She was silent for so long he was already steeling himself for a refusal when she said, "It took me a while to find a place I like. How attached are you to your apartment?"

He felt a surge of hope. She'd been to his apartment and she knew it was nothing but a basic box with a kitchen and bathroom. "Not at all," he said. "If you'd like to keep this place, I could give up my apartment and move in here with you."

She was silent again, and he caught himself nervously jiggling his leg, a habit he'd outgrown in about the eighth grade. Was she going to say no?

He cleared his throat. "Is it such an awful suggestion that you don't know what to say?"

She didn't laugh, as he'd hoped. "It's a big step," she said seriously. "May I have some time to think about it?"

"Sure." He swallowed the urge to insist that she let him move his recliner in tonight. He made a production out of checking his watch, waited five seconds. "Was that long enough?"

"Very funny." She wrinkled her nose at him, hesitated, then spoke again. "Sam, it's not that I don't want you—"

"I'm aware of *that*," he said dryly.

She couldn't hide her smile, but she kept speaking. "—but you're talking about something that's sort of permanent."

And marriage would be even more permanent.

Marriage? The idea had lain just beneath the surface of his thoughts for a while now, he realized. If he and Del were going to be together long-term, he wanted her to marry him. Wanted to know she'd be his forever. He was a little surprised at the rush of satisfaction the notion gave him. Del. His. Forever.

Yeah, he liked it. But apparently, she wasn't feeling quite the same way, judging from her reaction to his suggestion of merely moving into a place together. He hated to think of how she'd have reacted if he'd asked her to marry him. "What if we did it on a trial basis?" he said. Mentally, he said goodbye to the notion of moving his furniture anytime soon.

"That might work," she said. "Like a month and then see if we still think it's working?"

He shrugged, feigning indifference. "A month would be a good start."

"And you wouldn't give up your place until then, at least," she added.

He didn't like the sound of that, but figured he'd worry about his lease in a month. By then, maybe he could convince her that living together—forever—was a good idea.

* * *

Monday morning had been underway for exactly two hours when the thing he'd been dreading for years occurred.

The phone rang in the outer office. He barely noticed it. The phone rang all the time, but Peggy took the calls, routing them to whoever they were meant for.

A moment later, though, her voice came over his intercom. "Sam, line one is for you. She wouldn't give her name, just said she was a potential client."

"Thanks, Peg." He pushed away from his keyboard and punched the button on the phone system, taking a moment to stretch. "Sam Deering, may I help you?"

"Don't you mean Sam *Pender?*" It was a woman's brassy tone. "I'm calling for *PEOPLE* magazine. Are you the Sam Pender who stopped that gunman in San Diego?"

It shook him. How in the hell had they found him? He'd been so damn careful, had sealed the records of his name change and even changed his social-security information. "Wrong last name," he said, reaching for brisk cheerfulness. "Sorry."

"We want to do a piece on you," the woman said

in a rush. "A sort of where-are-they-now kind of thing. We'd need to—"

"Sorry," he said again, firmly. "I'm not Sam Pender." *Anymore.* "If you require the firm's services, please call again."

He punched the button to end the call. Then he clasped his hands before him on his desk, noting only distantly that they were actually shaking, for God's sake. Publicity. He'd evaded it for seven years. How had they found him? Or had the journalist been fishing, adding a few facts and hoping they equaled the right answer? Maybe that was all it was.

He drew a breath and spun around again to face his monitor. The company had just gotten a kidnapping case that was going to require coordination from several of PSI's departments, since it involved European travel and recovery of an American national in another country. Not to mention getting the child safely away from the noncustodial parent.

He shook his head briskly to clear it. He had other things to worry about. That phone call probably had just been a fishing expedition. No way could they be sure it was him.

After work, he had to go by his apartment to pick up clothes and a few other things he thought he'd need next week. Del went straight to her town house because, she said, she wanted to wash her hair and let it dry by itself. If she used a hair dryer it would get too frizzy.

He'd never noticed Del's hair looking frizzy in seven years. It must be a woman thing, he thought as he unlocked his door. Either that, or in seven years she'd never used a hair dryer a single time.

His apartment had a faint air of disuse. It should. He had hardly been here except to pick up his mail and occasionally grab some clothes since he'd been with Del the first time. And it was going to stay that way if he had anything to say about it.

The answering machine was blinking and he crossed the room to press the button and play the messages. The first one was from his mother in Nebraska. He'd call her tomorrow and give her Del's number. He imagined his mother would jump up and down at the thought that he was living with a woman. She'd be dreaming of more grandchildren with no encouragement at all. While he was at it, he'd better caution her about the reporter who'd called. His family protected his identity but it was best not to be blindsided.

The second was from his sister, reminding him of his niece's fourth birthday. Thank God she also had some suggestions for gift ideas because he didn't know squat about little girls.

His dentist's office had left the third message. It was time to schedule his six-month checkup.

The fourth was from Robert Lyon. He stood in shock as the cool, elegant, masculine voice floated into the room. He hadn't seen Robert in over a year. What were the odds of the man calling mere weeks after Sam and Del, the two people he'd introduced, had become lovers? Uneasily, he wondered if the man had ESP as he listened to the message.

"Hello, Sam. It's Robert Lyon. I'm in town for a few days and thought you might have time for dinner." He named the hotel where he was staying and left his number. Sam stood staring at the phone, then picked up the handset and punched the callback button. He knew from the little Del had spoken of Robert that she was fond of him. It would be a pleasant surprise for her if he took her out to dinner with Robert.

Del agreed to go out on Wednesday evening for dinner as easily as he'd anticipated. But he didn't tell her they'd be meeting Robert.

That night, she wore the little black dress that

had changed their relationship. He'd finished dressing ahead of her and gone out to the living room to check his e-mail on the laptop he'd brought over. He was just closing the program when Del walked into the room.

"Whoa," he said. "I like it even better the second time around."

Del smiled, tossing her long, unbound hair back from her shoulders. "I thought you might."

"Come here." He beckoned but she shook her head.

She knew what he wanted; he could see the heated awareness in her eyes. "No. We'll be late."

"So?" He stood, beginning to walk slowly across the room.

She backed away, putting the table between them. "Sam, we have reservations for seven!" The sentence ended in a shriek as he feinted left, then moved right when she dodged. He caught her by one elbow and whirled her to him, clasping her against him and running his hands over the silky fabric of the little dress and her curves beneath it. "I wanted to do this that night in the bar."

"You did?" There was amusement in her voice, but beneath it he detected a hint of vulnerability. Del had hidden herself away for so long she honestly didn't know how appealing she was.

"I did." Dropping his head, he sought her mouth and her resistance died as he plunged his tongue deep, finding her breast with one hand and covering the plump mound with one hand. He rotated his palm, the rising peak beneath his hand fueling his growing arousal. Her arms wound around his neck and her fingers speared into his hair, holding him to her. "Mmm," she murmured. "I guess we can have a quick appetizer."

He wanted her again. Badly. Tugging the hem of the dress up one smooth thigh inch by inch, he could feel himself growing harder and readier by the second. As he slipped his fingers beneath the little dress and around her thigh, he ground himself against her soft mound. Pulling her one leg high around his waist, he pressed himself even more intimately against her. He thought he might just die of pure pleasure. He trailed his fingers along the rounded globes of her bottom and the sweet crease he found until he touched her there in the heated V he'd exposed.

And holy heaven, she wasn't wearing any underwear!

"What…?"

"I wanted to surprise you." She tore her mouth from his and nipped his earlobe, then sucked hard on the tiny sting. The small sensation shot straight through his throbbing body, making his pants uncomfortably tight.

"Consider me surprised." He could barely get the words out. He released her for a moment and shoved his hands between them, opening his pants and pushing them and his briefs out of the way.

She was making tiny mewling sounds, trying to climb his body, and he obligingly lifted her, breath surging in and out of his lungs like a winded marathoner as her legs clasped his hips and her moist, heated female flesh caressed him.

"Inside you," he managed. "I need to be inside you."

She suckled his ear again. At the same time, her small hand burrowed down between them and she wrapped her fingers around him, sliding up and down gently as her thumb whisked over the ultrasensitive tip.

He almost lost it right there as she continued to caress him. Gritting his teeth against the urge to simply let himself relax and go with it, he gripped her soft buttocks in his big hands and lifted her higher, rubbing her over him.

She made a small sound of delight, her hand faltering in its task as he angled her against him so that she would feel as crazy as she was making him.

She moaned and clutched at his shoulders as he turned and braced her against the wall. He was almost ready to enter her when he realized he hadn't used protection, and he swore.

"Wait! We can't—"

Del made a shocked sound as he set her down and fumbled in the pile of clothes around his ankles until he came up with the small package he sought. He covered himself with frantic haste and then, with one slick, swift motion, he lifted her and positioned himself again, then thrust inside her. She was hot and wet and smooth and tight; he was out of control, pounding toward the pinnacle of his pleasure. She made a small noise with each motion of his hips, her body impaled by him, and he realized she was as close as he was. "Come to me, baby," he said hoarsely. "Let go and come to me."

"Sam," she said, her voice trembling. Her fingers dug into his skin as he felt sweet internal contractions begin to ripple through her. Her body arched; her heels dug into him. He threw his head back, shuddering as he felt his own body gathering, and then he couldn't think at all, could only feel as her body gripped him like a hot, tight glove, squeezing an earthshaking response from him that left his knees trembling and his entire body drained. Slowly, he dropped to his knees on the floor, still holding her.

"Wow," she said. "I'm not sure I'll be hungry for the main course."

He laughed, savoring the sweet intimacy of their position. "It's possible the main course will be delayed for a while after that." He lifted her off him, then staggered to his feet. "I'm not sure I can walk."

"I'm the one who should be saying that," she pointed out, reaching for the box of tissues on the counter. "Let me," she said when he reached for one.

Her fingers were soft and gentle as she cleaned him. By all rights he shouldn't be able to get hard again for a week after that. But amazingly, he felt a renewed stirring of desire beneath her hands.

"We really do have to go," she said, smiling.

"I know." He began to restore his clothing to order. "But I can't seem to tell *him* that."

She laughed aloud. "I'll be ready in a minute," she said as she walked toward the bathroom. "I'll hurry."

He glanced at his watch. "We're not late. You even have time to put on some underwear." He couldn't wipe the silly grin off his face as she rolled her eyes at him, then disappeared through the door. Satisfaction invaded his every pore. He'd needed that, to bond her to him, to make her his again. At least, he was sure of one thing: she still wanted him as badly as he wanted her.

So badly that you almost forgot something important, pal.

The voice in his head snapped him back to reality with a jarring thud. Holy hell. Birth control. The thought hadn't entered his head until he'd been poised and ready to take her. Unbelievable. If he'd ever known such a total loss of… He'd always thought he'd have kids someday, but after Ilsa had informed him she couldn't live with a man in a wheelchair for the rest of her life, he'd put that dream away. The fact that he wasn't wheelchair-bound was inconsequential; he simply hadn't wanted to get involved with anyone again.

Now, though, the thought of seeing Del with a baby—a baby they'd made together—was unexpectedly appealing. Apparently he hadn't buried those dreams as deeply as he'd assumed.

The moment they entered the restaurant, a tall, silver-haired man rose from a table where he'd been waiting and waved at them.

"Robert!" Del's voice held delight and amazement. "What are you doing here?"

Robert smiled as he embraced her, then shook Sam's hand. "I'm in town for a few days and when I called Sam, we thought it might be fun to surprise you."

"You were right." She smiled at Sam. Then she appeared to realize that Robert didn't know about them, and her whole face pinkened.

"Sam tells me you two are dating or something," Robert said as he held her chair and smoothly seated her.

"Or something," Sam said as the men sat.

Robert grinned. "So how's business?" he asked.

The meal was pleasant. They spent most of it discussing PSI in generalities, since confidentiality was a hallmark of the business. Robert knew a few of their clients because he had recommended them, but he was equally interested in some of the other work the firm had begun to do.

"I had good preliminary talks with a German firm that trains dogs for protection work," Sam told him. "We've had so many requests to add guard dogs to the security measures we offer that Del and I thought the time had come."

"We flew to Germany and visited three training

centers," Del added. "One clearly offered a superior product and they're interested in working with us. Essentially, we'd act as a middleman. When dogs are requested, we'll bring them straight from Germany to the client's home. We're adding a trainer to our staff who will evaluate all requests. If they're approved, he'll travel to Germany to transport the dogs. He also will stay with the client for a few days to ensure the proper setup is in place and there's someone responsible for the dogs."

Robert whistled. "Sounds like a big step."

Sam shrugged. "It is and it isn't. We offer every other type of home security on the market, but some people still feel more secure with dogs around."

"I can understand that," the older man said. "Evvie wouldn't be without our two."

Evvie was Robert's wife. They'd been married shortly after Sam had met the man and he'd also met Evvie on one or two occasions. A pretty, youthful-looking woman of about Robert's age, Evvie was a horsewoman and a dog person, as well. The couple had two large Dalmatians.

"How is Evvie?" Del asked. "She was getting a colt ready for the Preakness last time I talked to her."

"She's still horse-mad," Robert said with a

smile. "She recently invested in a new colt who's a several-times-great-grandson of Man O' War and she has high hopes for the Triple Crown."

Del's eyebrow rose. "Those *are* high hopes."

"Wish her luck from us," Sam said as the waiter appeared to remove their salad plates.

After the main course, Del rose and excused herself to freshen up. The moment she was out of earshot, Sam turned to Robert. "So I understand you know Del's mother."

Robert smiled, but there wasn't real humor in it. "I ought to. I was married to the woman."

"You're kidding." Sam was stunned. He tried to imagine Robert and the sort of woman Del's mother clearly was, and failed. "Before Evvie."

"Well over a decade ago. It didn't last two years," Robert said. "And the only reason it took that long for me to decide to leave was because I was brought up to think one never quit working at a marriage." He sighed. "But she wouldn't meet me halfway. Hell, she wouldn't even take the first step." He shook his head, and to his surprise, Sam detected a fond note in his voice. "She was a spoiled brat, but she could charm the socks off any man she met. Still can, for that matter."

"You're on good terms now?"

Robert nodded. "Once she got over the fact that for once *she* hadn't been the one to call it off, we were able to be civil. She's even had dinner with Evvie and me a time or two."

Dinner with Robert and Evvie? This was getting stranger and stranger. "What attracted you to her?" Sam asked, still trying to fathom Robert's interest.

Robert looked at him. "You're kidding, right?"

Sam shook his head.

Robert smiled. "Del's personality is very different from her mother's. Imagine Del dressed to kill, fluttering her eyelashes and deliberately aiming all that sex appeal at you."

"Ah." Sam smiled wryly. "It probably wouldn't have taken us seven years to get together."

Robert laughed. "Yeah. I could barely remember my own name." He took a sip of wine. "So tell me about you and Del."

Sam shrugged, picking up his own wineglass. "We've worked together for a long time. One day we realized we had…good chemistry." The understatement made him smile.

A moment later he realized Robert was regarding him with less than enthusiastic regard. "Del is a wonderful young woman," Robert said softly, "and I would do my utter best to tear your heart out if you hurt her."

Sam would have laughed except that Robert's blue eyes carried not a hint of humor. "I'm not planning on hurting her," he said evenly.

"At the risk of sounding paternal, might I ask what your intentions are?"

Holy hell. The man was serious. "I, ah, consider my relationship with Del to be a permanent one," he said, feeling his way through the minefield that suddenly had developed, "and I hope to convince her to marry me eventually."

The steely expression on Robert's face eased significantly and his eyes warmed again. "I see. Del isn't keen on marriage?"

Sam shook his head. "She doesn't even want to talk about next week, much less anything permanent. I've convinced her to let me move in on a trial basis, but that's it."

"Del hasn't seen many examples of successful marriages," Robert said regretfully. "But keep after her. I imagine you'll get an 'I do' one of these days."

Del returned then and both men stood. She eyed them curiously as she slid into the booth. "You two look guilty," she said. "Keeping secrets?"

Sam laughed. "When was the last time I managed to keep a secret from you?"

She smiled demurely. "True."

But he *was* keeping a secret from her, and his amusement faded as he thought of the phone call he'd received. Someone wanted to find Sam Pender, and if he wasn't careful, the quiet life he'd created for himself was going to be blown right out of the water.

After coffee, they rose to leave. Del preceded the men from the restaurant and Sam put an arm around her waist as they crossed the parking lot. At the car, Robert kissed her before Sam put her into the passenger seat and closed the door.

As he rounded the hood, Robert kept pace with him. "Thank you for bringing Del along. It was wonderful to catch up with both of you."

"No problem." Sam stopped and held out his hand. "I can tell Del adores you. Thanks for joining us."

Robert smiled as he clasped Sam's hand. "If you ever talk her into marrying you, let me know."

Sam nodded. "Don't hold your breath. She's still pretty skittish." He glanced fondly at the small woman sitting in his vehicle. "But I'll wear her down eventually."

Robert followed the direction of his glance and raised a hand in farewell when she waved at him. "Does she know you love her?"

Sam paused, going still. "I didn't say that."

"You didn't have to." Robert clapped him on the back. "I recognize the signs."

Sam opened his mouth to respond. But what, really, was there to say? He watched as Robert walked across the lot to his dark rental sedan and drove away with a final wave.

He loved Del. And Robert had seen it before he, Sam, had even been able to admit it to himself. The mere thought made him literally begin to sweat.

He *did* love her. Her quirky eyebrow and the baggy clothes she often wore, that stupid baseball cap and the way she impatiently flipped her braid back over her shoulder. Her ready sense of humor and her quiet stubbornness when she thought she was right. Her firm no-nonsense approach to handling their employees and the warmth he didn't have that she brought to the company.

His chest felt too small to contain his swelling heart as he stood there with his car keys gripped in his hand and his whole world sitting there five feet from him.

God, when he'd thought he'd been in love with

Ilsa, it had been a manageable, controllable emotion, subject to his will. When she'd left him, he'd been a little hurt, but a lot humiliated and even more angry that she would desert him when he most needed someone.

Loving Del wasn't manageable at all, he realized. If she ever left him, he would be devastated. His pride wouldn't even come into play, and perhaps that was the most telling thing. Abruptly, he spun and yanked open his car door, sliding into his seat and turning to Del.

She was looking at him with a humorous question in her eyes, but he couldn't explain. Leaning across the console, he cradled her head in both hands as he set his mouth on hers, kissing her with all the tenderness of the feelings rolling through him.

When he finally lifted his head, her eyes were soft and dreamy. She touched her lips with one finger. "What brought that on?"

He shrugged as he inserted the key into the ignition and turned on the engine. "Nothing in particular. I just thought you needed kissing."

It was her turn to lean over the console as she kissed him on the cheek. "You thought right."

He smiled as he put the car in gear and started home. He'd lied when he'd said nothing in particular. He might love Del, but he wasn't stupid enough to tell her so. As cautious as she was, she'd head for the hills before he could get out the third word.

No, it was going to take time to woo her, to make her see that she couldn't live without him, either. To make her relax those ever-present guards around her emotions and love him back.

Time. It wasn't as if he was going anywhere.

Seven

In the middle of the night, he woke up sweating. His heart was pounding, adrenaline rushing through his system as the remnants of the dream receded.

Damn. This was the second time in less than a month.

Del was sitting up in bed beside him, one hand lightly clasping his arm. "Hey," she said. "You were having a bad dream."

After the first time, he'd had the dream over and over again, whenever he closed his eyes. Only in the dream, sometimes the gunman turned and pointed his weapon at Sam before he could get to the guy. It had been months before he'd gotten a decent night's sleep. As the years had passed, though, it had ambushed him less and less frequently, so much so that now he was surprised when it recurred.

"Want to tell me about it?"

He hesitated. He still wasn't ready to tell her all about his past. Being called a hero made him cringe. He'd only been doing what he'd been trained to do that day; he'd known he had a moral obligation to try to stop that killer.

But if he was going to continue to be with her she deserved to have some explanation.

He pulled her down into his arms, enjoying the way she instantly softened and draped her body over his. "It's a recurring dream. I've had it for almost eight years now."

"It has to do with your injuries, doesn't it?"

"Yes." He stroked her back, absorbing the silky texture of her smooth skin. Somehow it wasn't as hard as he'd expected to talk about this with her, lying here in the dark, quiet room. "But I wasn't wounded in combat."

"Then how did you get shot?" Her voice was intense and puzzled. "Those *are* gunshot wounds."

And she would know. One of their bodyguards had been winged a couple of years ago, and just last year a member of the abduction team took a bullet in the thigh while reuniting a little boy with his custodial parent after he was taken out of the country by the other parent.

He took a deep breath. "I got shot by a nut job on the street. It was kind of ironic—I'd never been wounded in combat, but a day after I get home on leave, I get nailed right on the street." That was all true. It just wasn't the whole truth.

"This one—" she lightly touched the puckered scar above his left hip "—must have done some damage."

"It nicked my spine," he said tersely. "I spent a couple months at a rehab center."

"Rehab center?"

"Learning to walk again." He could feel the muscle clenching and unclenching in his jaw. "For a while they thought I was going to be paralyzed. I had no feeling in my legs for about three weeks."

She gasped and her hands moved in an unconscious gentling circle on him. "No wonder you have nightmares. That must have been terrifying."

"It was. Luckily it only lasted a short time." He

dismissed the fear and abject terror, the budding despair of those three weeks with one sentence.

"I'm so glad you weren't permanently paralyzed." She stretched up to kiss his chin, then lingered, pressing light, soft kisses against his throat and working her way down his chest until she found one small, flat nipple.

He forgot his somber thoughts as pleasure instantly ricocheted through his body. Del didn't seem to want to talk, didn't seem to need additional explanation. And that was fine with him.

Way more than fine. She was soft and warm and eminently arousing as she squirmed into better position atop him, and he found himself swiftly, completely aroused, hard and full and aching for the sweet oblivion she promised. He reached down and pressed against her inner thigh until she parted her legs on either side of his body.

He sucked in a raw breath of need as he grabbed protection from the bedside table. "Wait a sec," he growled as he deftly covered himself. Then he moved into place, inching himself into her at an excruciatingly slow pace. When she moaned and wriggled, trying to push herself down onto him, he held her hips in his big hands and kept it slow and leisurely.

"Sam," she pleaded, "please…please…"

"Please what?" With one quick move, he rolled them so that she lay beneath him. The motion had nearly dislodged him, and her hips surged restlessly as he braced himself above her and resisted her urgings.

"Please…" She was panting, her fingers digging into his hard buttocks as she tried in vain to pull him closer.

"Please…this?" He lowered his weight onto her abruptly, driving his hips forward, embedding himself deeply within her as she arched up to meet him, her arms tightening as if to hold him there forever.

"Yes." The word was a bare whisper of delight.

He looked down at her, silhouetted in the moonlight that shone through her window. Her dark hair was a wild spill across the pillow. Her eyes were closed and her lips were full and soft from his kisses, lightly parted now with passion.

God, she was beautiful. And she was his.

He and Del were meant for each other, meant to spend the rest of their lives together. They complemented each other in so many ways. He couldn't imagine his life without her, couldn't predict a future that didn't have her in it.

He was determined to have her in his life.

Now all he had to do was convince her. She was wary and as skittish about commitment as he'd been just days ago, but he was going to change that, he vowed. He was going to marry her.

The following week, Del popped her head into his office toward the end of the day and said, "We're celebrating Beth from bookkeeping's birthday this evening. Do you want to go?"

He hesitated. *No* was on the tip of his tongue but he wanted to spend the evening with Del, and he supposed this was her indirect way of telling him she planned to go. "I guess since I went to one, it might cause ill will if I didn't go to them all now," he said with a grimace. "Right?"

"Probably," she said in a cheerful voice. "It would be a nice thing to do, too."

He stared at her. "I am not nice."

She laughed. "All the more reason for you to go and be civil."

Which is how he found himself sandwiched between Del and the new woman, Karen, at a round table in a small Italian restaurant, singing "Happy Birthday" to Beth from the bookkeeping department. They had just finished the song when the door to the restaurant opened and Walker entered.

"Sorry I'm late," he said. "Happy birthday, Beth."

Sam felt both Del and Karen stiffen. It was hard to miss, smashed between them as he was in the bench seat. Women, he supposed, had an internal radar for relationship trouble. And that was what had just walked through the door.

Walker had the top-heavy, intellect-light redhead with him again. His tie was crooked—very— and the redhead's lipstick was smeared across one cheek. Her hair looked as if someone had set off a small explosion beneath it. There was little question what the pair had been doing. God, he hoped he and Del were never that obvious.

Both of them looked as if they'd had more than a few drinks. Even if Karen had divorced Walker a long time ago, it probably still was no fun seeing your ex make an ass of himself with a woman young enough to be his daughter.

"Thank you," said the birthday girl. "Pull up a seat."

Walker grabbed a chair from a nearby empty table one-handed, swiveling it around so that he could sit. Then he grabbed the redhead and tugged her down onto his lap, winding a brawny arm about the girl's waist as she giggled. "Jennifer, everybody," he said, waving a hand. "You met some of them before. Everybody, this is Jennifer."

"Hi." Jennifer waved like a beauty queen on a parade float. She turned to Walker. "Which one is Karen?"

"That would be me." Karen raised her hand, her voice cool and casual.

Jennifer examined Karen for a long silent moment, then turned to Walker. "You said she was old. She's *pretty*," she said in a sulky voice.

Walker looked as though he'd swallowed his tongue. "Sorry," he mumbled, and Sam wondered if he was talking to Jennifer or Karen.

Around the table, curiosity was as strong a presence as the new guests. No one else in the company, other than Del and he, knew Walker and Karen Munson had been married once, as far as Sam knew.

At his side, Karen stirred and spoke into the uncomfortable silence. "Could you excuse me, please? I need to get going."

She stood and Sam stood automatically, pushing Del before him so they could let Karen slide out of the seat.

She paused at the edge of the table and smiled

at Beth. "Happy birthday," she said. "Thank you for inviting me."

"We do it all the time," Peg said. "You'll soon be good and sick of us inviting you to celebrate birthdays. We might as well just glue this on our thighs." She indicated the piece of chocolate cake on her plate.

There was a general ripple of agreement and a few chuckles, and Karen smiled again. "See you tomorrow."

She was already turning to walk away when Jennifer-the-redhead said, "Why's she leaving? I thought you said she didn't have a family anymore." Although she was speaking to Walker, the words carried across the table.

Karen stopped abruptly. "Pardon me?" She turned back to the table, her face carefully expressionless.

"Well," said Jennifer, "Walker said you didn't have a husband or a kid anymore, so—"

"Jennifer, shut up," Walker growled.

Karen looked as though someone had punched her in the stomach. Tears sparkled in her eyes, but after one scathing glance at Walker, all she did was smile again at Beth, though her lips quivered. "I hope the rest of your evening is wonderful," she said. One tear trickled down her cheek but she didn't wipe it away before she turned and walked steadily out of the restaurant.

"Well," said Peggy brightly, "I think it's time we all headed out, don't you?"

Subdued murmurs of agreement greeted her words, and the table was suddenly a flurry of activity as people gathered personal items and rushed off. A few of them cast dark looks in Walker's direction as they left.

"Dammit, Walker," said Sam, "that was completely out of line."

Jennifer spoke. "Sorry," she said in that ridiculous baby-doll voice. "I didn't mean to hurt her feelings."

"Of course not," said Del in a voice that left no doubt of her opinion.

"If she can't take the heat," Walker said aggressively, "she should get out of the fire."

Whoa. Now he'd done it. Sam had been around Del long enough to know when the match touched the fuse. It didn't happen often but when it did, there was no stopping her.

Del leaned forward, her expression set in stone. "That's *kitchen,* you moron. 'Get out of the *kitchen.*'" She stood, almost shaking with fury. "You had no business sharing Karen's personal difficulties with that twit." She didn't even look at the redhead as she slid her arms into her jacket and picked up her briefcase. "Your life," she added in an icy tone, "is your own business. But when you inflict someone on us who's so offensive that she can ruin an entire evening in one sentence, it becomes *our* business."

She stood, then jabbed Jennifer in the shoulder with a stiff forefinger. "If I ever see you at a PSI party again, I will pull out every fake red hair on your empty head."

"And you." She transferred her attention to Walker. "Don't bother coming to any more of the office parties unless you're sober and single."

Walker was glaring at Del, a muscle in his jaw ticking uncontrollably. "Sam?" he said, not looking away from her angry face.

Sam sighed. "She's right. You showed up and everyone left. That ought to tell you something." He put an arm around Del, feeling the anger vibrating through her as he hustled her out of the restaurant before she completely lost her temper. He didn't really want to have to bail her out on assault charges.

He held her car door until she settled herself with rigid, angry motions, then climbed into the driver's side and started the engine without speaking. A smart man knew when to keep quiet. As he drove out of the lot beside the restaurant, he could feel Del still simmering.

Finally, about halfway home, he said, "Every fake red hair on her empty head?"

There was a moment of tense silence and for a minute, he thought she might be about to take *his* head off. Then Del snickered. "I thought it was fairly poetic."

He laughed aloud. "That wasn't quite the first word that sprang to mind."

"So what was?"

"Sincere," he said, "It sounded like you meant it. I think if I were Jennifer, I might not be anxious to cross your path again."

Del sobered quickly. "I can't believe that bimbo said that. I *really* can't believe Walker was dumb enough to tell her that he was married to Karen once."

"And believe me, I'm sorry I mentioned it to him."

"You should be," Del said seriously. "That's personal information and we don't have any right to talk to anyone about it. You think she'll quit?"

"I hope not. Frankly, I'd sooner fire Walker than lose her. She's been working her butt off this week, and she's about ten times as diplomatic as Mr. Foot-in-Mouth has ever been."

Sam grinned. Walker did have a reputation for telling it the way he saw it. They didn't often let him deal directly with clients. "I hope we don't lose either one of them."

Del was quiet for a moment. "Why do you suppose she ever married him?"

"I imagine he had his good points at the time."

"I guess." She sighed.

"People can be deceptive," he said, thinking of Ilsa. "A little chemistry can blind you to someone's less-charming traits."

From the corner of her eye, he caught the abrupt motion of her head as she turned toward him. "You sound as if you have firsthand experience." It wasn't a question and yet he knew it was.

"I was engaged once."

· He heard her suck in a sharp breath. "But not married?"

"No." He was glad he was driving. It was easier than facing her when he went through this story. "She changed her mind pretty fast when she thought she might be stuck with a paraplegic for life."

"I'm sorry," she said quietly.

"It was no big deal," he said. "If she wasn't

going to stick, better I found out before the vows."
But when he glanced over at her, her brown eyes
held a well of sympathy, and he suspected she
didn't believe his profession of unconcern. "I can't
even remember what she looked like anymore," he
said, and was surprised to find it was true. Since
he'd gotten involved with Del, the past had faded
into insignificance.

"Still, it must have hurt when she cut and ran."
There was anger in her tone.

"Look," he said, feeling cornered, "I'm sorry I
didn't tell you before—"

"I'm not mad at you!" Her eyes went wide with
surprise. "I'd like to rip her heart out, though."

Amazingly, he was able to laugh again. Ilsa really *wasn't* important anymore, and the knowledge was like emptying his pockets of a load of
rocks. "Your bloodthirsty side is showing tonight."
He reached over and laced his fingers through hers,
drawing her hand onto his thigh. "Lucky for you,
I like bloodthirsty women."

Her hand turned over in his, then slipped down
between his legs and a jolt of electric sexuality ran
up his spine. He wanted to whimper aloud when
her fingers began to explore, and he felt himself
begin to pulse and fill. "Lucky for you," she said,

her fingers exploring the growing bulge behind his zipper, "this bloodthirsty woman likes you. In fact—" she glanced down at the evidence of his desire for her, plainly outlined in the khaki pants he'd worn to work "—she can't wait to get home."

He gave a hoarse laugh which turned into a moan as his zipper opened with a soft hiss and she slipped her hand inside. "Much more of that and we won't make it home."

The next morning at work, he couldn't ignore the buzz of gossip in the hallways. Everyone was talking about what had happened the night before. If he heard, "I had no idea they used to be married!" once, he heard it a dozen times.

Karen had puffy dark bags beneath her eyes, but she worked with the same efficiency he'd begun to notice she brought to all her tasks, presenting him with a study of the manpower it would take to covertly watch a home in Rio where a client's child was believed to have been taken by her noncustodial ex-spouse.

Around three o'clock, he was standing beside Del's desk going over flight reservations for a visit to the German canine people to finalize the deal, when Peggy appeared in Del's doorway with a vase of flowers. "Check it out," she said. "Karen got flowers!"

"From who?" Del went around her desk and tried to look at the card but the tiny envelope was sealed.

"Don't know. But I already called her to come get them, so we won't let her leave until she spills the beans," Peggy said cheerfully.

Sam snorted, and both women looked at him.

"What was that for?" Del asked.

He shook his head, grinning. "No reason. I just don't get what the big deal is."

Peggy shot him a pitying look. "Receiving flowers is *always* a big deal."

Karen stuck her head in the door at that exact moment and both women turned to her, but Sam remained rooted to the spot where he stood. Guilt, strong and forceful, rushed through him.

He'd never given Del flowers. Hell, he'd never even taken her out to dinner unless it was work related. He'd intended to, but somehow they always seemed to get sidetracked by a mattress when they weren't working.

In fact, that was pretty much *all* they did, he thought with a pang of regret. They worked, ate and fell into bed together. They damn near burned up the sheets every night, and neither one of them had gotten enough sleep since her birthday, but he wasn't complaining.

And neither had she. He wondered if she really didn't mind the fact that he'd never once taken her on a real date. If she did, she hid it so well he'd never caught a hint.

"What's it say? Who's it from?" He tuned back in to the conversation as Peggy began to pester Karen.

With an odd, frozen look on her face, Karen silently passed the card over to Peggy.

"That rat bastard!" Peggy wasn't shy about voicing her opinion.

Del, crowding over her shoulder, said, "At least he realized he was way out of line."

Karen didn't say anything. She just stood there, holding the vase of pretty pink-and-lavender flowers with a blank, bewildered expression on her face. Sam reached out and snagged the card from Peggy, reading the simple message.

I'm sorry. Walker

"Hey," said Peggy, "You okay, honey?"

Karen sighed. "As okay as I'll ever be with that jerk on the same planet," she said. She shoved the arrangement back at Peggy. "You can keep these. Brighten up your office. Pitch 'em. I don't care."

She turned and started toward the door, then turned back and plucked the card from the arrangement. "But I think I'll keep this. Just to remind me he isn't a complete and total waste product."

Sam was pretty impressed that she managed a smile in response to Peggy's and Del's laughter before she left the office.

Eight

He lay on his back in bed that evening with Del curled against his side. Her fingers idly combed through the hair on his chest and he decided that with very little effort he could be persuaded to make love to her again. But first, there was something he wanted to do.

"What do you think," he began, "about dinner and a movie on Saturday night?"

Her fingers stopped moving. After a moment, she said, "I think lots of people probably will be doing that."

He slid his hand down over her hip and pinched her backside. "Smart-ass."

"Hey!" She lurched against him before settling back down with a grin. "Oh, did you mean what did I think about the two of us having dinner and then going to a movie?" she asked with false innocence.

"Or I could invite some other girl."

"Not if you want to have any shot at sleeping in this bed again." They both chuckled, but her casual words warmed him.

That was the first time Del had ever alluded to a future of any sort. She was generally extremely careful about *not* defining their relationship, to the point that for the past couple of weeks he felt as if they'd been dancing around some enormous piece of furniture, pretending it wasn't there.

"So," he said, "would you like to go out?"

Del turned over and levered herself above him, propping her arms on his chest. "I would love to," she said, as her hair fell around them in an intimate curtain, "but may I ask what prompted this?"

He shrugged. "I just thought it would be fun."

She digested that for a moment. "Yeah," she said softly, "it would be fun. We don't take much time for just enjoying ourselves, do we?"

"Outside of this bed?"

She smacked his chest with the flat of her hand.

He captured her hand and pulled her down closer. "You're right. I think it's time we started to think a little more about getting to know each other outside the bedroom."

"Or the office," she added.

He smiled, running a hand over the smooth hair that spilled down around them. "Yeah."

She laid her head on his chest. "Dinner and a movie would be nice." She paused. "Your heart is beating really fast."

"My heart always speeds up when you're around," he said without thinking.

Del went still.

He realized what he'd said. Oh, hell.

Then he felt her body relax against his again. "My heart beats faster when you're around, too," she said softly.

He was so relieved that for a minute he couldn't speak. And by the time his vocal cords were functional again, he'd let it go too long, so he didn't say anything.

But long after her breathing slowed and evened out as she slipped into sleep, Sam lay awake wondering. What had she meant? Had she only been thinking in physical terms or had she understood that he'd been speaking of emotion?

They slept in the next morning until nearly ten. Unlike most of the Saturdays they'd spent together, he awoke before she did. He put on some coffee and grabbed a quick shower, then stepped into a pair of jeans before heading back to the kitchen. Pouring a cup of coffee for himself and one for her, he carried them to the bedroom.

After setting the cups on the bedside table, he bumped her hip with his until she grumbled and slid over far enough for him to take a seat on the edge of the mattress. Del wasn't a morning person, he'd discovered with some amusement. Until she'd had a cup of coffee, there was no point in even trying to hold a conversation or expect her to frame a coherent answer.

"Good morning." He braced his hands on the mattress on either side of her body and leaned down to nuzzle her throat, seeking out the warm, sweet woman fragrance he'd discovered was strongest there. When her arms came up around his neck and she arched her body up to his, he smiled against her skin. "I have coffee."

Immediately, one arm left his neck, hand outstretched. "I am your slave forever."

Forever. He liked the sound of that. A lot. And he wished she meant it, but he suspected it had simply been a trite phrase. Well, that was okay. He had plenty of time to make her see how good they would be as husband and wife.

He was flipping eggs when the shower cut off and he grinned in satisfaction. Perfect timing.

Then the doorbell rang.

Puzzled, he automatically headed for the entryway. Who in the world could be at Del's door? She appeared to have no close friends and didn't do anything other than work that he'd been able to see.

He checked the peephole, but could only catch a glimpse of an artfully tousled blond head of hair and a bit of a woman's profile. Relatively satisfied that whoever it was presented no imminent threat of physical harm, he flipped open the dead bolt and turned the knob.

"Darling!" The woman came at him with her arms outstretched, then halted abruptly. "Well," she said, smiling coquettishly. "You're not the darling I had in mind, but you'll do." She let her gaze drift over his bare torso. "You'll do quite nicely." Then her smile sharpened as she dropped the vamp act and she held out a hand. "You must be Sam. It's wonderful to finally meet you."

He couldn't have spoken if his life depended on it. He'd recognized her the moment she'd turned to face him.

Aurelia Parker. *The* Aurelia Parker!

The woman standing before him was one of Hollywood's darlings, an actress who'd been making men drool since he was old enough to spell the word *woman.* Possessor of an Oscar and a couple other awards he couldn't name, a nominee several times, a guaranteed box-office star worth millions, Aurelia Parker had to be nearly old enough to be his mother but she looked hotter than a lot of women his own age in a slim black pantsuit beneath which a simple white shell showed a surprisingly decorous hint of cleavage.

Silently, he held out his hand.

The actress took it and he was surprised by her firm, no-nonsense grip.

"I am," he finally said. "Sam." Wow, that was brilliant. He cleared his throat and stepped back. "Please come in." *And tell me what the heck you're doing here and how you know my name.*

She gave him a dazzling smile. "Now I see why Del has kept you to herself for so long. I was so thrilled when I heard about you two. I had begun to despair of her, I tell you." One finely arched eyebrow shot up. "I know I shouldn't ask, but Del will never tell me. Is there any chance you two are thinking of starting a family soon?"

Huh?

"Sam, don't answer my—" Del stopped dead in the entrance to the living room, her face a study in shock and dismay. All she wore was a large navy bath towel wrapped around her, with a smaller white one wrapped turban-style around her wet hair. The bloom he'd put in her cheeks earlier vanished instantly as she took in the scene. "Mother. Hello."

Mother? Aurelia Parker was Del's mother?

Now he knew what the expression *thunderstruck* meant because that's exactly how he felt. As if he'd been struck by a bolt from the blue. Only that would be lightning-struck, wouldn't it?

He supposed that single arching eyebrow should have been a clue, he thought, immediately recalling the expression. And just what the hell had Del told her mother—*good God, could Aurelia Parker really be her mother?*—about the two of them? He'd been under the impression that Del and her parent rarely talked, but apparently Del had confided in her sometime during the past few weeks when he wasn't around. Which wasn't often.

"Hello, dear!" Aurelia Parker crossed the room and threw her arms around her daughter. "Happy belated birthday! I hadn't seen you in so long I thought it would be lovely to surprise you."

"But I told you this weekend didn't suit," Del said in a tone that would have frozen a polar bear.

Aurelia Parker straightened her shoulders, her feathers clearly a little ruffled at Del's reaction. "If I waited until it suited you, I'd be in a nursing home." The voice was crisper than anything he'd ever heard her utter on the screen, and for a moment, mother and daughter simply stood and measured each other.

Studying the two women, their resemblance was startling, although their differing styles played down the similarities. Someone who wasn't looking for it might not even realize they were related.

But to him, it was clear. Del's chin was a little more determined, and she mostly ignored her assets while her mother enhanced her eyes, her lips, her skin and damn near everything else that he could see to the maximum. Their figures were similar although her mother seemed a bit top-heavy considering how petite the rest of her was. Then again, that probably was the result of a clever bra or surgery.

"Fine. Come on in and make yourself at home." Del's voice was resigned. She seemed to have recovered a little, but even through the anger that was rapidly replacing his shock, Sam could see that she was deeply upset. "I've asked you never to drop in without calling, remember?"

"But, darling, it wouldn't have been a surprise if I'd called! And this way, I got to meet your adorable Sam. He's been out of town every other time I've come by."

Out of town? What other times? He looked at Del, who was even paler than she'd been when she'd first seen her unexpected guest.

"Uh, Mom—"

"Honestly, Del." Aurelia glanced at him and smiled, then turned back to her daughter. "I thought I was never going to get to meet your husband."

Husband? It was a good thing Aurelia wasn't looking at him, because his mouth fell open.

"Mom, make yourself at home," Del said hurriedly. "Sam and I need to get dressed." She snagged his hand with the one that wasn't holding her towel in place and towed him toward the hallway that led to the bedrooms.

He let her, not because she actually had any hope of moving him, but because getting Del alone seemed like the quickest way to find out exactly why in the hell Aurelia Parker thought he was married to her daughter.

Del dropped his hand the second they stepped into her bedroom. Crossing her arms defensively and hugging herself, she said, "I guess you'd like an explanation."

"You mean I'd like to know why your mother—whom you neglected to mention is a world-famous actress—believes you're my wife." His voice cracked like a whip and he saw her flinch. But hell—all he could think of was what a disaster this was. He'd spent seven years in blissful anonymity, and the first time he took a full-time lover she turned out to be the daughter of a star who rarely went a day without making some publication somewhere. What were the chances that he was going to stay anonymous now?

Hell, he'd even been thinking about marriage. Wouldn't that have been just peachy?

"I needed a husband," Del blurted. Her color was coming back in a big way as her cheeks flamed with what he could only assume was embarrassment at being caught in her lies. "Not a real one. Just a fictional one to get her off my back and make her stop trying to set me up with every man she came across."

"So you used me." He couldn't control the rage and hurt seething beneath his set expression.

"Well, yes." She looked completely ashamed. "It was easier if I talked about you than if I completely made a guy up. This way, I didn't have so many details to worry about, since I already knew you."

"How long?"

She didn't pretend to misunderstand. "Almost six years now. She thinks we have an anniversary coming up in two weeks."

"Hell!" He raked a hand through his hair. Aurelia Parker was Del's *mother.* He'd be lucky if there hadn't been tabloid photographers outside Del's door this morning taking pictures of him in his unbuttoned jeans.

Del flinched again at the succinct curse. "I didn't think you'd ever really meet," she said, her voice shaking. "I mean, it wasn't as if…"

"We were lovers," he finished grimly. "Didn't it even occur to you *recently* to tell me who your mother was?"

Tears were standing in her eyes now. "Yes. No. Oh, I don't know. I've spent my entire life trying to get away from being Aurelia Parker's daughter. I was afraid if I told you, you'd…look at me differently or something. Or not want to be with me at all."

He was too angry to be careful with his words. "You're damn right about that. The last thing I want is to be hooked up with someone whose name is going to get in the papers."

Del put a hand to her throat, a blatantly defensive gesture, but her voice was steadier when she spoke again. "You have something specific against fame or is this just a general policy?"

Ah, what the hell. He'd been going to tell her soon anyway. "Eight years ago I stopped a gunman on the street in San Diego before he killed more people. I spent the next year trying to get away from the publicity it generated."

"The San Diego shootings," she whispered. She looked absolutely stunned. "He killed seven people before he was stopped by a Navy SEAL on shore leave. That's *you?* Sam Pender?"

"Was," he corrected. "I even had to change my name."

"Why? You should be proud of the lives you saved that day."

"I am," he said. "But I didn't need all the hoopla

that came with it. I was just doing what I was trained to do. What I *knew* I needed to do to stop that guy." He shook his head, looking into the past. "At first, there were reporters all over the hospital where I'd been taken. They would have followed me to the rehab center if I hadn't changed my name—"

"They said you would never walk again," she said, almost to herself. "They were wrong."

"Yeah, and the last thing I want is to have to start running from the press again."

"Oh, Sam, I'm so sorry." Del looked stricken, but he was too angry to care. She slumped down onto the edge of the bed, her lower lip trembling. "I'll go out and explain to her that I've been lying to her. You can leave if you like. I wouldn't blame you if you did."

He turned away from her and paced the room. "Why in the *hell* didn't you tell me?" He was repeating himself in his agitation.

This time, a hint of the Del he knew emerged. Her spine straightened. "Why didn't you tell me your secret?"

"I was planning to!" he roared, and she flinched. "If you'd been straight with me from the beginning—"

"I didn't think it was any of your business in the beginning," she flared. "We might be sleeping together but that doesn't mean I have to share my life story with you."

The words hit him with the force of a blow. He stopped moving, his back to her as he absorbed the implications of her terse response. Clearly, she hadn't been seeing their growing closeness in the same light he had. In her mind, all they were doing was sleeping together. She couldn't have made her position more clear.

"You're right." His voice sounded stiff and rigid even to him; he had to force the words out through a throat so tight he could barely speak. "It isn't any of my business."

There was a silence behind him as he stalked over to the dresser and yanked out an old university sweatshirt, his standard Saturday attire. As he tugged it over his head, she said, "Sam..." in a trembling voice.

But he was done with the whole mess. "I'm leaving," he said. "You can tell your mother whatever you want."

He slammed the bedroom door behind him and snatched his keys off the kitchen counter as he headed for the door.

Del's mother half rose from the couch where she'd taken a seat. "Sam...."

He didn't bother answering.

He didn't know where else to go, so he went to the office. It was pretty damn pathetic, he thought, when a man didn't have a single friend he could call on at a time like this. But it was true. He'd immersed himself in his business so deeply that even his family had been excluded gradually. It had been too painful to stay in touch with his buddies still in the teams so he'd let their overtures and persistent calls go unanswered until they'd finally given up.

Del was the only other person who knew him anymore. Under normal circumstances he might have considered calling Robert, but this situation was far from normal, and besides, Robert couldn't be expected to be objective. The man might not be related to Del by any legal or biological means, but it was clear that he was the closest thing she had to a father figure.

And Robert had been married to Aurelia Parker. *That* was going to take a while to compute.

As he let himself in and reset the security system, he berated himself for being four kinds of an idiot. He almost snorted aloud as he thought of how wrong he'd been in his mental vision of Del's mother.

Your mother didn't want kids?
She was afraid they'd ruin her image.

What an ass he'd been! He'd assumed she meant that her mother was worried about regaining her figure and still looking young. He'd half feared her mother had been a hooker, dependent on her looks for her income. When, in fact, Del had literally meant that a child might ruin the sexpot image Aurelia Parker projected as her stock-in-trade.

God! He threw himself into his executive chair and spun around to face the window. What the hell was he going to do now?

What did it matter? He doubted Del would keep his identity from her mother, and even if she did, what were the chances he could hang around Aurelia Parker's daughter without everyone in the world seeing him? Someone would eventually recognize him, and then he'd be right back to that crazy place he'd been in eight years ago, with women everywhere angling to meet him. He knew how the reality-TV bachelors felt—the only differences were that he hadn't chosen to make himself America's bachelor, and he hadn't gotten a million dollars for it.

Just one hell of a lot of aggravation and a total loss of privacy.

The beeping of the security system interrupted his thoughts, and he swiveled his chair back around, moving the mouse so that his computer monitor screen saver vanished and the programs were visible. Clicking on the state-of-the-art program, he saw that Walker's ID had been confirmed by the scanner that surveyed his employees' irises.

Moments later, he heard the subdued *whoosh* of the elevator doors opening and Walker's footsteps marched across the carpet toward his office. Hell. The last thing he wanted to do was put on a pleasant face today.

"Hey, boss." The big man loomed in the doorway. He leaned a shoulder against the frame and crossed his arms. "Thought I'd be the only one in here today."

"Nope. Beat you to it." He didn't feel like answering questions so he asked one instead. "What are you doing in here on a Saturday?"

Walker shrugged. "I wanted to check over the plans for the child-recovery op next week one last time, be sure we've got contingency plans to cover every sort of foul-up." He shifted from one foot to the other and his gaze slid away from Sam's.

And suddenly Sam thought he knew what was eating at the guy. Karen Munson was going undercover on that op.

"She's going to do fine," he said quietly. "Her references are terrific. I wouldn't send her if I wasn't confident of her abilities."

"I know." Walker didn't pretend to misunderstand. "I just want to be sure nothing goes wrong."

Sam nodded.

"I mean, I've been thinking…" Walker's eyes met Sam's. "I'm not sure putting Karen on cases involving kids is such a good idea. If something ever goes wrong, she's going to take it hard."

The man might have a point. "But I can't pick and choose her assignments," he said to his buddy.

"I guess not." Walker sighed. "She knew coming in that a lot of recovery work deals with kids."

"She did."

"And it's not my job to worry about how she's handling that."

"It's not," Sam agreed.

"It's just that…she's hurting," Walker said. He looked thoroughly ashamed. "I've already hurt her more. And I don't want to add to it."

"I don't, either, but I can't just yank her off every case involving a kid, with no explanation. Everyone else would see what was going on and they might resent her getting special treatment." He met Walker's gaze with a cool one of his own.

"Most of them don't know about her past. Or they didn't before the other night."

Walker's face turned a dull brick-red. He put up a hand and massaged the back of his neck roughly. "I was an idiot," he said. "You probably should have fired me."

"I thought about it," Sam said honestly.

"The thing is," Walker said, "she said she loved me. But when we couldn't agree on our lifestyle, she bailed. Couldn't get away from me fast enough. I couldn't let that go."

"And now?"

Walker sighed heavily. "And now I have to face the fact that I've destroyed any chance at a relationship with the only woman I've ever loved." He let his arms drop to his sides as he slowly straightened. "Guess I'll check over a few things before I take off." He aimed a halfhearted wave in Sam's direction as he moved off down the hallway toward his own office.

Nine

Now I have to face the fact that I've destroyed any chance at a relationship with the only woman I've ever loved.

As Walker's footsteps receded down the hallway, Sam sat frozen in his chair.

God, was that what he, Sam, had done? He'd lashed out at Del, worried about himself rather than thinking about her feelings. She hadn't told him about her mother at first because she hadn't wanted to lose him. She'd probably been afraid— and with good reason, given her past—that he'd be happier with his connection to the famous star than he was with her daughter. How could she have known how the news would affect him? A sense of shame crawled through him. She hadn't been the only one keeping secrets. Why should he have expected her to trust him more than he had allowed himself to trust her?

But…he *did* trust her. With the sparkling clarity of hindsight, he saw that over the past seven years, he had trusted Del with far, far more of his company's intimate workings and secrets than any mere employee normally would warrant. He'd always known, in his heart, that she would never betray him. Long ago, something in him had recognized that she loved him, even though she'd always been careful and correct in his presence.

She loved him! Realizing that should have made him the happiest man in the world. But he'd screwed up royally when he'd walked out on her. She'd needed him, he saw now. Needed a buffer between her mother and her. She'd created an artificial one over the last few years with their fictitious marriage, but now, when she needed protection the most, he wasn't there.

Abruptly, he surged to his feet, rolling his chair back so hard it banged against the wall. He had to get home and apologize. He didn't want to be

Walker, screwing up his life so thoroughly that he could never straighten it out with the one woman he really loved.

As he headed down to his truck, he thought of Del and his confidence returned. She loved him. She had to, or she couldn't be so tender, so responsive. She couldn't finish his sentences and read his moods unless she was totally tuned in to The Sam Channel all the time, just as he was able to discern her thoughts before she opened her mouth half the time.

She loved him! And it went both ways. He hadn't been ready to recognize or define his feelings for Del before, although he didn't really know why. He'd already acknowledged the fact that Del was very different from Ilsa. If she had a self-centered bone in her body he had yet to see it.

Something contracted in his heart as her face came into his mind again, a certain knowledge he'd never felt before with anyone. He loved her, and he'd better get back there and tell her so.

But…when he did see her again, what was he going to say to her?

Marry me. The answer was right there in front of him, and it was so simple he was amazed he hadn't seen it before.

They'd tell her mother the truth, and invite her to the wedding. He almost smiled when he thought of telling Del he wanted to make her marriage real. She was wary and cautious about relationships, but he'd already bulldozed over most of her fears. He'd just tell her she didn't have a choice.

Once, he'd thought Ilsa had cured him of any desire to put a ring on a woman's finger. By now, though, the betrayal and hurt he'd once felt had altered, become nothing more than thankfulness that he'd escaped such a shallow relationship. It wasn't marriage he'd been avoiding, he'd realized. It was putting your heart in someone else's hands.

Now he was ready to hand Del his heart in a wrapped box.

He stepped into Del's apartment fifteen minutes later, filled with anticipation. If her mother was still there, he'd apologize. He'd grovel, if that was what it took to get Del to forgive him.

But as the door swung open, there were no voices. No lights. No smell of the scented candle Del loved and faithfully burned whenever she was at home. The apartment felt empty, and he knew before he even called her name that Del wasn't there.

Maybe she'd taken her mother to her hotel.

Maybe they'd gone shopping. He reached for acceptable alternatives to the terrible fear that was spreading through him.

Behind him, another key scraped in the lock and the fear began to ebb. He whirled—but it wasn't Del who stepped through the door. It was Robert, looking unusually grim.

"Hey," Sam said. "What are you doing here?"

"Get your things and give me your key to this place." Robert's face was granite hard, his tone far less than friendly.

Sam was stunned. "Where's Del?"

"She asked me to come over in case you returned," Robert said. He handed Sam a plain white envelope.

With a sense of foreboding, Sam tore it open and extracted two sheets of paper. Del's familiar handwriting covered the top page.

Sam—
Enclosed is my resignation, effective immediately. I'm sure you'll find someone to replace me quickly. Sorry to leave this way, but I can't imagine working together anymore. I'm sure you agree.

Again, I apologize for not being straight with you.

Thank you for making my first love affair so very special. I will treasure the memories always.
Del

Every little sliver of radiance that had begun to shine in his heart dimmed and went out. She'd thought he wasn't coming back. Because in her world, when people ended a relationship, it was over forever. They moved on.

And now she'd moved on, too.

God, please don't let it be too late. Their relationship was barely beginning. It couldn't end like this.

He reread the note, disregarding Robert's chilly stare. *Love affair.* He clung to that small phrase as if it were golden. She hadn't called it a "sexual encounter" or even simply an affair. She'd called it a love affair.

"No," he said. He ripped both sheets of paper in half and let them flutter to the floor, focusing on Robert again. "She's not leaving the business and she's not leaving me. Where is she?"

Robert shook his head. "Don't ask me that."

"I *am* asking, dammit!" he roared. "I want her back."

"Why?" Robert was watching him closely.

"Because…" He floundered, reluctant to expose his newly discovered feelings. This was between him and Del. "Because I do."

Robert shook his head. "Not good enough. You can find another reliable employee."

"I don't care about the work," he said harshly. "I want *Del*."

"Again," Robert said, "why?"

The hell with his stupid concerns. If he had to shout his feelings from the rooftop in order to get her back, that's what he'd do. Sam cast Robert a furious glance. "I love her. That's what you want to hear, right? Well, there you go. I love Del."

Robert's frozen expression relaxed and he almost smiled. "It's not me you need to convince."

"Then tell me where she is and I'll tell her, too." He didn't care if he begged. "Please, Robert. I have to find her. I hurt her feelings and I wasn't fair to her. I need to apologize." He swallowed, and for the first time he truly realized that there might not be a future for him with Del. "Even if she doesn't want to come back, I still need to apologize."

Robert hesitated. Finally he said, "She went to Aurelia's hotel. They're planning on flying out in the morning."

"Flying out where?"

"Back to California."

Shock rippled through him; he had trouble taking a deep breath. "She doesn't belong on the West Coast. And she hated living with her mother. Why would she go back?" Panic was making it hard to get the words out.

The older man shrugged. "What is there to keep her here?"

Sam winced.

"Apparently she and her mother had an honest talk. Aurelia's a forceful personality: I don't think she realized just how she intimidated Del as a young child. This was the first time she ever really understood just how much Del hated having men thrown in her path all the time. Aurelia wanted Del to be happier than she's been. It might sound misguided to you and me, but she honestly thought she could help Del meet the right man."

"And instead it pushed her away. Clear to the other side of the country." He felt even worse. It had taken Del years to come out of her shell and take a chance on him. He looked at Robert. "What hotel?"

Thirty-five minutes later he was at the exclusive hotel in the heart of the capitol where Aurelia had commandeered the most luxurious suite they had to offer.

Robert had given him directions to the hotel as well as the suite number, and he strode to the elevators and rode up to her floor without incident. His heart was pounding as if he'd run the miles from Fairfax.

He'd considered calling to let her know he was coming, but he was afraid she'd leave again. When he knocked on the door, he stayed well out of range of the small peephole through which she might look.

"Who is it? Aurelia isn't here at the moment."

He supposed he was glad she was cautious, and smart enough not to simply open the door to anyone, but now the moment of truth had arrived. What if she refused to talk to him?

He cleared his throat. "It's Sam," he said. "I'd, ah, I'd like to talk to you, Del. Please," he added belatedly.

Silence. Not a single sound issued from her side of the door.

"Del?"

"Go away." Her voice was tight. "I don't have anything to say to you."

"Then you don't have to talk." He attempted to keep his voice low and reasonable.

No answer.

"I'll talk. All you have to do is listen."

Again, silence.

"Let me in," he said forcefully, "or I'll stand out here and yell until you do."

The words were barely out of his mouth when the locks clicked and the door swung inward. "Be quiet!" she hissed. "There are probably journalists camped in every room around here waiting to report something about my mother."

"If you'd let me in when I asked nicely, I wouldn't have had to shout," he pointed out as he moved forward.

Del skittered backward and he caught the door with the flat of his hand before it could hit him. Gently closing it behind him, he followed her down a wide hallway toward a sitting room.

She was wearing jeans and a T-shirt but they weren't the baggy kind she wore at work. These were clothes she'd bought in the weeks since their first night together, clothes that showcased her slim figure, the jeans hugging the curve of her bottom. Her hair was down, gently swaying as she moved, and he closed his eyes briefly, undone by the mere thought of never having the right to run his hands through those marvelous, silky tresses again.

He forced himself to concentrate on his surroundings when he realized his hands were actually shaking. On the right were bedrooms, on the left, a dining room and a powder room. Holy cow, this was an entire apartment. All it appeared to lack was a kitchen and he wouldn't be surprised if there was one of those, as well.

For one swift, surprising moment, the differences between his own barely middle-class ranch upbringing and her far more luxurious one loomed large between them and he almost faltered. It shocked him a little. He'd never thought himself particularly class-conscious, but Aurelia Parker's wealth was pretty damn intimidating.

Then he remembered that Del had left all this behind. She lived in a modest apartment—by these standards, anyway—worked at an average job and did her own errands and chores. She lived like him. No one ever would have guessed at her silver-spoon beginnings. She didn't want, didn't need wealth to make her happy. He hoped to God he was right in thinking he knew what would.

Del had taken a seat in an armchair near an enormous black-marble fireplace. He took another and pulled it forward so that he was sitting mere inches from her. She didn't actually move away, but her averted eyes and the way she seemed to curl herself into the smallest shrinking ball imaginable spoke loudly enough.

He didn't know how to begin, so he said the simplest thing. "I'm sorry."

Her forehead wrinkled and for the first time since she'd met him at the door, she met his gaze squarely. "*You're* sorry? But I lied—"

"I lied, too. By omission if not literally." He took a deep breath. "I didn't think about how you felt. I didn't understand."

Del linked her fingers together. She looked away again and he saw her chin quiver before she pressed her lips into a tight line.

"Will you tell me about it?" he asked quietly. "Your childhood?"

Again, she didn't speak, and he realized she was trying not to cry.

Pain cleaved a hot wound through his heart. He'd caused this.

"From the things you said about your mother," he prompted, "I thought she might be a hooker."

He got a reaction: The Eyebrow quirked in response. "A hooker?" She almost smiled, but it faded fast. "No. She was just a lot more preoccupied with her career and her image and her love life than she was with her child. You know she's been married four times, right?"

He shook his head. He wasn't much for keeping track of celebrities' lives. He had enough trouble with his own. "Wow."

"And there were a lot of wannabe Mr. Parkers in between them. My father, Pietro Caminito, was her first husband. After he was killed, she married and divorced three more times." She went on without waiting for his response. "She wasn't a bad mother, not abusive or anything like that."

He remembered what she'd said about the parties. "What about the man who almost attacked you?"

She shrugged. "Mom was having a cast party after one of her films wrapped. Everyone was supposed to be outside, but this guy was wandering around inside the house. I had come out of my room to see if I could watch the party from the upstairs gallery windows." She took a deep breath. "I was looking out the window when he grabbed me from behind."

Sam couldn't prevent the deep, primitive sound that rose from his throat as he thought of a young Del, defenseless against an adult male.

"Robert stopped him," she said quickly. "He was my stepfather at the time. I think it's the first and only time I've ever seen him really, really furious. He knocked him down and called the cops. My mother had the guy arrested and she swore he'd never work in the film industry again. And she never had another house party without hiring bodyguards to keep people in the party areas."

Sam snorted. "But she didn't stop having parties."

Del smiled faintly. "No. Are you kidding?"

There was a short silence between them.

"You changed your last name," he said abruptly. "Why Smith?"

"It was my grandmother Parker's maiden name, except she had an *e* on the end," she said. "I didn't want anyone to treat me differently because of who my mother was so I had it changed legally." She shook her head. "Mom thought I couldn't possibly be happy without a husband. You can't imagine how many potential spouses she tried to tempt me with." She made a doubtful face. "Like I was supposed to want to get married after watching her all my life."

He supposed, between watching her mother bounce from husband to husband and growing up in the false environment of Hollywood, that Del had good reason not to believe in marriage.

"It's not that I don't love her," Del said. "She's

not a witch. She just didn't get it for a long time. That's…that's why I made up a husband." Her brown eyes were wide and earnest. "Sam, I never would have involved you on purpose. I had no idea she was coming to town. If I had known about the San Diego shooting…"

"We both had our secrets," he said, "and good reasons for keeping them."

She nodded, but her gaze had slid away again and her face was a lovely, remote oval. Her shoulders moved slightly in a helpless gesture. "At any rate, I'm sorry, as well." She seemed to think the subject was closed.

"So you'll come back?"

Her eyes flew to his, and he thought there was a flicker of hope amid the pain and sadness there. Or maybe that was just wishful thinking, because she shook her head. "No."

Well, okay, Sam, stop dancing. She's gone for sure if you don't say something. At least this way you'll know you tried. He took a deep breath. "You don't have to come back to work if you don't want to, but I want you to stay."

She started to shake her head but he leaned over and put his hand over hers, and she froze.

"Marry me," he said. "I need you. I've needed

you for years and I was too dumb to figure it out. Since the night of your birthday, my life has been perfect. Well, almost. If you marry me for real, it really will be perfect."

Del's eyes were huge, riveted to his now.

"Say something," he blurted. "If you can't stand the thought of marriage, we can just live together."

He read the refusal in her eyes before she spoke. "I can't, Sam." She rushed ahead when he tried to break in. "I appreciate the offer, but I couldn't do that to you. Do you know how your life would change if people found out...?"

"I've been thinking about that," he said urgently. "If I'm married I won't be exciting anymore. Besides, being a hero is nothing to be ashamed of."

Del shook her head, smiling pityingly. "Maybe not, but together, the hero of San Diego and Aurelia Parker's daughter would generate some headlines. Don't kid yourself about that."

"It won't last long. We'll let your mother take us out to dinner and get it over with. We'll be old news the second the next Hollywood starlet gets engaged."

But she didn't smile, didn't say anything. Her expression was both sad and skeptical.

Desperation rose. She was so close, and yet she

might as well have been on the moon. "Del, I *want* the world to know we're married. We can live in a glass bubble as long as we're together." And then he realized what he'd forgotten. "I love you."

She actually pulled away from him. "You don't have to say that." The tears were back, trembling on the brink of her lower lashes.

"I'm not just saying it." He leaned forward, took her hands again, noticing with distant disinterest that his own were still shaking. "I love you, Del. If you can look me in the eye and tell me you don't love me back, I'll walk out of here now." He took a deep breath, tried to smile although it felt crooked and pathetic. "It might kill me but I promise I'll leave you alone."

One single tear spilled over and trickled down her cheek. "Oh, Sam, are you sure?" she whispered.

That surprised a laugh out of him. "Sure it would kill me? Yeah," he said. "I'm sure. I've seen the way Walker and Karen still eye each other when they think the other isn't looking. I don't want to mope around like that for the rest of my life, wishing I hadn't ruined my chance at a life with you. I want my ring on your finger. I want a house, a dog, even some kids if you think you could deal with that."

"Children…"

"But I'm flex on that," he said hastily. "I want *you*. I love you," he added again, "and that's all that matters to me."

She took a deep breath and suddenly launched herself forward into his lap. "I love you, too," she said, wrapping her arms around his neck in a stranglehold. "Oh, Sam, I love you, too."

Relief rushed through him, so strong he would have dropped to his knees if he'd been standing. He pulled her close, burying his nose in her hair, running his hands up and down her slender back. "I thought I'd lost you," he confessed, knowing his voice was shaky and not caring.

"I thought you didn't want to be with me anymore after you found out who my mother was and how it might affect your life." She ran her fingers through his hair and pulled back to smile at him. "I'm so glad I was wrong."

"Is that a *yes?*" He still wasn't sure enough of her to assume anything.

"Yes." Perched on his lap, she gazed into his eyes. "To marriage, to kids, to all of it."

"Thank God." He almost sagged with relief.

"I could never imagine being married except to you. I dreamed of it for so long and told myself it would never happen, I guess I was afraid to let myself hope."

"Now you don't have to hope anymore."

She smiled, nodded, dashed away a tear. "I promise we'll do our best to stay out of the spotlight."

He shrugged. "We'll deal with it. And it won't last. We're not exciting enough."

She tilted her face up to his. "You're plenty exciting enough for me," she told him, her voice going low and husky as she pressed herself against him.

Sam lifted her into his arms and started back down the hallway. "Is one of these bedrooms free? You haven't seen exciting yet, babe."

Del laughed, pointing to a doorway. "That one." She put her hand against his face, the look in her eyes so loving and tender that he actually felt his heart stutter. "I love you, Sam. Why don't you show me how exciting we can be together?"

Epilogue

The flight to Las Vegas with Del's mother hadn't gone as badly as he'd feared. Aurelia Parker Caminito Haller Lyon Bahnsen could carry a conversation with minimal help from another person just fine.

She had told them all about the movie she'd just made, and the recent parties she'd attended. She'd talked about who was rumored to be doing illegal substances and who was currently in rehab. She'd talked about Del's father, the Italian race-car driver who'd died in a frightful, fiery accident on a track in Europe in front of thousands of horrified onlookers, and about husbands two and four. Husband Number Three, Robert, sat across the cabin from them with a laptop open in front of him, oblivious to his former wife's chatter. He'd called his wife, Evvie, before they'd left and she was catching a flight, planning to meet them at their hotel before the service.

A Vegas wedding had been Del's mother's idea, largely because the lack of preplanning wouldn't alert the media. That held some appeal. But it had appealed to Sam because he didn't want to wait one day longer than necessary to marry Del.

He couldn't imagine his life without her now. Not waking with her in his arms in the morning, not watching TV at night with her nestled in his lap, not bumping into each other in her small kitchen as they made a meal. Not ever feeling her smooth, silky skin again, never parting her legs and finding her warm and ready for him, never sinking into her so deeply he felt as if they were one.

Thanks to the vows they'd just exchanged, he never would.

Holding Del's newly ringed hand in the small, amazingly tasteful chapel Aurelia had found, he glanced down at his bride yet again, feeling the familiar shock of love, attraction and tenderness welling up within him.

She was radiant in a simple white-satin gown that caressed her curvy body and swept to the floor to trail behind her. A circlet of pearls and shining beads crowned her loose, flowing hair and a sheer white veil floated down from it to kiss the hem of the gown. Her mother had worn the ensemble when she married Del's father—the only white gown she'd ever worn, she pointed out—and when they'd announced their plans and the idea of the Vegas wedding had taken shape, Aurelia had had the dress overnighted to the hotel. It was there when they arrived, along with a seamstress who did some minor alterations so that it fit Del like a second skin. He still couldn't quite wrap his mind around the advantages that truly amazing amounts of money could provide. Thank God, Del didn't seem to care about it.

"Right over here," the minister said, interrupting Sam's preoccupation. "If you'll just sign the marriage license, we'll be through here."

Oh, boy. He took Del's elbow and steered her toward the table. "You first."

His new bride signed her name in the firm, rounded script with which he was so familiar. Then she straightened and handed him the pen.

He bent over the legal contract. He blinked as he looked at Del's signature and started to chuckle.

She glared at him, balled her fist and hit him solidly in the shoulder. "It's not funny."

"Oh, but it is." Laughing even harder, he bent and signed his own name, then laid the pen down. "Don't those look nice?" he asked her.

The Eyebrow rose at the inane question. "Lovely," she said dryly.

"Look closer," he suggested.

She shot him a puzzled glance, then focused again on the marriage license. "What's the big deal?" She glanced over the form, then her gaze drifted down and she read their names. *"Are you kidding me?"* She was already starting to laugh.

He shook his head. "My parents named all their children from the Old Testament. It's my given name."

Del was shrieking with laughter and the minister was regarding them as if they might need to be hauled away in straitjackets. Robert, Evvie and Aurelia hurried over to examine the license, and a moment later they all were laughing like a pack of hyenas.

"What are the odds…?" Del was still chuckling.

He shook his head. "No way could this happen again in a million years."

And as he took his new bride's hand and they started into the rest of their life together, he cast one final glance at the marriage license in his hand.

Delilah Aurelia Smith, it read. And on the line for her new spouse to sign: *Samson Edward Deering.*

* * * * *

Look for Anne Marie's next book,
THE HOMECOMING,
part of Silhouette Books's Logan's Legacy
continuity, in May 2005.

Silhouette® Desire®

Coming in December 2004

The Scent of Lavender series continues with

Jennifer Greene's

WILD IN THE MOMENT

(Silhouette Desire #1622)

The whirring blizzard, the cracking fire and their intimate quarters had Daisy Campbell and Teague Larson unexpectedly sharing a wild moment. The two hardly seemed like a match made in heaven...so why couldn't Daisy turn down Teague's surprise business deal and *many more* wild moments?

The Scent of Lavender

The Campbell sisters awaken to passion
when love blooms where they least expect it!

Available at your favorite retail outlet.

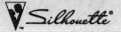